W9-CSA-233

L A S T
LAUGHS

LAST LAUGHS

THE 1986 MYSTERY WRITERS OF AMERICA ANTHOLOGY

EDITED BY

GREGORY MCDONALD

THE MYSTERIOUS PRESS • New York

The Mysterious Press, 129 West 56th Street, New York, N.Y.
10019

Printed in the United States of America
First Printing: June 1986
10 9 8 7 6 5 4 3 2 1

Library of Congress Cataloging-in-Publication Data

Main entry under title:

Last laughs.

1. Crime and criminals—Fiction. 2. Detective and
mystery stories, American. 3. Humorous stories,
American. 4. Horror tales, American. I. Mcdonald,
Gregory, 1937-   . II. Mystery Writers of America.
PS648.C7L37   1986   813'.0872'08   85-62061
ISBN 0-89296-246-1

ACKNOWLEDGMENTS

Mystery Writers of America and The Mysterious Press wish to thank the following authors and publishers for permission to include copyrighted material:

"Grief Counselor" by Julie Smith. Copyright © 1978 by Renown Publications, Inc. First published in *Mike Shayne Mystery Magazine*. Reprinted by permission of the author.

"Kindly Dig Your Grave" by Stanley Ellin. Copyright © 1970 by Stanley Ellin and the author's agent, Curtis Brown, Ltd., 10 Astor Place, New York, NY 10003.

"The Nine Best Movies" by Gregory Mcdonald. Copyright © 1986 by Gregory Mcdonald.

"I Do Not Like Thee, Dr. Feldman" by Henry Slesar. Copyright © 1969 by HMH Publishing, Inc.

"The Most Dangerous Man" by Edward D. Hoch. Copyright © 1972 by Edward D. Hoch. First published in *Ellery Queen's Mystery Magazine*. Reprinted by permission of the author.

"The Last Meeting of the Butlers Club" by Jeffrey Bush. Copyright © 1980 by Jeffrey Bush. First published in *Ellery Queen's Mystery Magazine*.

"Sidney, Seth, and S.A.M." by Charles R. McConnell. Copyright © 1986 by Charles R. McConnell.

"You Drive, Dear" by Fred S. Tobey. Copyright © 1961 by H.S.D. Publications, Inc. Reprinted by permission of the author.

"The Problem of Li T'ang" by Jeffrey Bush. Copyright © 1977 by The Atlantic Monthly Company. First published in *The Atlantic Monthly*.

"Hizzoner's Water Supply" by Gerald Tomlinson. Copyright © 1982 by Gerald Tomlinson. First published in *Ellery Queen's Mystery Magazine*. Reprinted by permission of the author.

"Light Fingers" by Henry Slesar. Copyright © 1962 by Fawcett Publications, Inc.

"It's All a Matter of Luck" by Tonita S. Gardner. Reprinted by permission of the author. Copyright © 1979 by Davis Publications, Inc. First published in *Alfred Hitchcock's Mystery Magazine*, October, 1979.

"Providence Will Provide" by Thelma C. Sokoloff. Copyright © 1980 by Thelma C. Sokoloff. First published in *Ellery Queen's Mystery Magazine*. Reprinted by permission of the author.

"Dogbane" by Frank Sisk. Copyright © 1972 by H.S.D. Publications, Inc. Reprinted by permission of the author's estate.

With special thanks to Michael Seidman and Bill
Malloy; and in appreciation to all MWA members
who generously submitted manuscripts even
before the shape and direction of this volume
were determined.

CONTENTS

L A S T
LAUGHS

THE LAST LAUGH

INTRODUCTION
BY GREGORY MCDONALD

The humorous crime story would appear to be a contradiction. How can crime be humorous? Crime is what we have declared by law to be offensive to us.

That *humorous crime stories* exist tells us something about ourselves.

A few years ago, I read one of those academic soothe-the-psyche papers, the theme of which was that all human tension develops from *the denial of expectations*. The car in front of you signals a right turn and suddenly turns left. Your heartbeat increases and possibly your blood pressure; you bang your horn at the other driver and possibly you question his intelligence. In your career you do not get the promotion you expected; in your marriage

1

your spouse does not love you in the way you expected. Tension, unhappiness, illness, according to this paper, are caused by one's having unrealistic and therefore frustrated expectations. As none of us is a perfectly successful prophet, our inevitable unhappiness and unhealthiness derive from our having any expectations at all.

Nowhere in this paper was it reflected that *the denial of expectations* is also a definition of humor. That the car in front of you signaled right, to a physical fitness center, but suddenly turned left, to an ice cream parlor, makes an amusing anecdote. Witty stories about employers' imbecilities abound. Much of literature, witty and otherwise, concerns the unpredictability of spouses.

Humor is in the telling. The key to *the telling* is the perspective. Tragedy is the fact, the death; drama is the interpretation, the life; humor is in the *distancing*, the refining of the fact, the interpretation, the frustration, the offense, the hurt, the anger not always to the point of approval, but at least acceptance.

Inevitably, there is a percentage of the population who cannot take their focus off the seriousness of any event. To tell the tragic or dramatic event wittily to these people is not to enhance an understanding or acceptance of the event, but to demean it. They love to pick their scabs. To these people I say, "Never be more than a city block away from your psychiatrist. You haven't the sophistication to survive on your own."

The humorous perspective is essential to survival.

Bursting with expectations, people come to America, move west, back East, South, North, from the cities to suburbs, from rural areas to the cities. It is not gold with which American streets are paved, but chewing gum. The fountain of youth dispenses soft drinks that rot the teeth.

So great are American expectations, so inevitably must such great expectations be denied, that immediately the American choice became clear: *laugh, cry, or get your gun.*

It's a choice, you see. And it's a good thing so many, some called fools, some called sinners, some called *humorists*, have chosen to maintain the wicked discipline of wit.

A crime is a tragedy. Someone has violated someone else, by robbery, rape, maiming, or murder. So tragic is the fact of any crime, of the willingness of one person to violate another, so dramatic are the ramifications to both the criminal (as victim) and everyone surrounding him, and to the victim and everyone surrounding him, that we are well served to develop, where possible, the perspective that permits us to accept the criminal event. In the tragic perspective, the tragic event is overwhelming; it stands as dominant as a mountain on a plain. In the dramatic perspective, the events to be interpreted are selected thematically; selected facts make a mountain range of peaks, some higher, some lower than others. In the comic perspective, the telling event is not permitted to overwhelm or be uneven with its environment; topographically, it is a mountain range worn down, refined, into a plain.

The tragic event, dramatically interpreted, is surrounded by *mitigating circumstances*. Yes, the car in front of you signals right and turns left; how annoying, but observe further, if you will, what the other driver is doing: he's changing his mind from exercising vigorously to eating ice cream; how amusing. What the other driver did remains stupid, dangerous, potentially tragic. We still do not approve of what he did. But the discipline of our perspective, our refinement, permits us to accept his stupidity better, to survive his crime more happily and healthfully.

Laugh and you'll live longer!

How do these members of the Mystery Writers of America in their short stories get us to laugh at that which isn't funny, accept behavior we have declared by law to be unacceptable, survive the tragedy of crime? The *mitigating circumstances* visible from their telling perspective are equal to the crime itself.

In Stanley Ellin's *Kindly Dig Your Grave*, an exploiter gets exploited. In Jeffrey Bush's *The Problem of Li T'Ang*, an imposter gets caught by a plagiarist. Charles R. McConnell, in *Sidney, Seth and S.A.M.*, and Fred S. Tobey, in *You Drive, Dear*, get us to accept and possibly even approve of revenge from the grave. The mitigating circumstances are such in Thelma C. Sokoloff's *Providence Will Provide* and Tonita S. Gardner's *It's All a Matter of Luck* that we find ourselves accepting the idea that society gets about what we deserve. Julie Smith's *Grief Counselor* is even more direct social criticism. In Gerald Tomlinson's *Hizzoner's Water Supply*, an antisocial act is committed about which society doesn't seem to care. *The Nine Best Movies* suggests how villains and victims sometimes seem to need each other. Henry Slesar's two stories, *I Do Not Like Thee, Dr. Feldman* and *Light Fingers*, describe something that happens to a character simply as a result of that character's uniqueness. And there are those stories that have fun with the mystery genre itself, Jeffrey Bush's *The Last Meeting of the Butlers Club*, Edward D. Hoch's *The Most Dangerous Man*, and Frank Sisk's *Dogbane*.

It is well to have expectations, lest we be immobile and not live life. One of our expectations must be that a goodly proportion of our expectations will be denied. At the happenstance of a denied expectation, if we permit the event to dominate, it is tragic; seen relatively, the event can be perceived as simply dramatic; refined absolutely into the context of life, with all life's mitigating circumstances, a comic, or at least ironic, perspective usually can be attained.

It is vitally important to have *the last laugh*.

JULIE SMITH

GRIEF COUNSELOR

started to give Sidney Castille my usual rappity-rap. "This is Jack Beatts," I said, "with the Grief Protection Unit of the county coroner's office . . ."

That was as far as I got before he hung up.

Sidney's wife, Dawn, had died two days before in a freak accident. He'd found her with a broken neck and her copy of *Vince Mattrone's 30-Day Yoga Actualizing Plan* lying on the floor beside her. It was open to the section on headstands.

I'd called him because it was my job. After the death certificates are signed, they're sent to me or one of the other grief counselors so we can get in touch with the victim's families.

As soon as Sidney hung up, I knew he was out of touch with his feelings. He was in the first phase of the grief cycle—what we psychologists call the stage of "disbelief and denial." He was refusing to deal with death.

That's normal and that's okay, but I wanted Sidney to know he had alternatives. I had things I could share with him. So I decided to pay him a visit.

I meditated a few minutes to get myself centered and then I drove my Volkswagen over to Sidney's house on Bay Laurel Lane. It was a typical northern California redwood house set back from the road in a grove of eucalyptus. Smoke was coming out of the chimney.

As I got closer, I could see the living room through sliding glass doors that opened onto a deck. Several cats prowled in the room like tigers in a forest. Dozens of plants hung from the ceiling and took up most of the floor space as well. There was nothing to sit on but oversized cushions.

On the far wall of the room was a fireplace with a pile of books in front of it. A man was squatting there, burning the books, feeding them one by one into the fireplace.

"Sidney?" I said. "I'm Jack Beatts from . . ."

"Oh, yes, the man from the coroner's office."

He let me in and waved me to a cushion, but he didn't seem pleased about it. In fact, he went right back to feeding the fire.

"Sidney," I said, "I'm going to be up front with

you. When you hung up, I sensed I'd better get over here right away."

"Yeah, that's what I thought. I guess I panicked when you said 'coroner's office.' "

"A lot of people are uptight about that. But I'm going to ask you to forget about the bureaucracy and just be open with me."

"I guess we may as well get it over with." He put a copy of *Zen Flesh, Zen Bones* in the fireplace and turned around to face me. A tear rolled down each cheek.

"That's it, Sidney," I said. "Flow with it. Experience your feelings."

"You talk like Dawn."

"I know how it is, Sidney. Everything reminds you of her, doesn't it? But that's okay at this stage. I don't want you to be negative about it."

"Negative!" he snorted. "What am I supposed to . . ."

"I'll bet those are Dawn's books you're burning." He nodded. "And it looks like you're about to take the cats to the pound. You're getting rid of everything that reminds you of Dawn, aren't you?"

Tears came into his eyes again. "I couldn't take it anymore, Mr. Beatts. I never should have married her in the first place."

"I know where you're coming from, Sidney. You felt inadequate because you were a lot older than Dawn, right?"

"She was twenty-two," he said, "and looking for

a daddy. A rich daddy. And I was just lonely, I guess. I picked her up hitchhiking on my way out here from Ohio after my first wife died." He winced. "But *she* died of natural causes."

"Death *is* natural, Sidney. I mean life is a circle, you know? I want you to choose to recognize that. And if burning books is what's happening for you, I don't want you to feel guilty behind it. Just acknowledge that it's okay."

"Look, are you going to take me in or what?"

"Take you in? Oh, you mean to the Grief Center."

"Is *that* what they call it in California?"

"For sure. We can rap anywhere you like if the vibes are wrong here."

"What is a vibe, Mr. Beatts? If I heard Dawn use that word once, I . . ."

"Now stay loose, Sidney. I hear what you're saying and I sense you're uptight behind it. You couldn't relate to Dawn's lifestyle, right?"

He began picking up cats and taking them to the carriers on the deck. I didn't want to blow the energy we had going, so I followed along beside him.

"She was all caught up in what they call the human potential movement," he said. "Transactional analysis, transcendental meditation, self-actualization, bioenergetics, biofeedback . . ."

"She must have been a heavy lady."

"She talked funny. Like you. And she cooked things like wheat germ soufflé. And she wanted the

house to be 'natural.' You couldn't go to sleep without a cat curled around your neck, or a spider plant
tickling your nose. It got so every time I saw her do
that crazy yogurt . . ."

"Yoga."

He closed the last carrier and we went back into
the house.

"I used to call it yogurt to annoy her," he said,
squatting by the books again. "Anyway, when she
started to stand on her head, she'd do it first with
her feet against the wall and then she'd let go of the
wall and stick her legs up in the air. Well, every time
I saw her with her feet like that, getting little
toeprints all over the paint, I'd think how easy it
would be just to grab her and . . ." He stopped.

"And what?"

"And snap her neck."

I nearly clapped him on the back I was so
relieved. At last he'd gotten his energy flowing in a
positive way! "I have to acknowledge you, Sidney,"
I said. "It's really a far out thing to see someone
being so open about his fantasies."

Sidney tried to speak, but he couldn't. He took
out a handkerchief and blew his nose. Sometimes
you have to hurt people to help them so I took a
chance.

"You killed her, didn't you, Sidney?" I said.

He kept his eyes down as he put the handkerchief
back in his pocket. "You knew all along," he said
finally.

"For sure," I said supportively. "Self-recrimination is very common in the first stage of the grief cycle and I want you to know that it's okay."

"Okay?" he said. "I don't understand."

"A lot of people get on that kind of trip when something like this happens. You and Dawn weren't getting along and you feel guilty about it now, right? You think she died because of something in your karma."

The way Sidney looked at me I could tell he was surprised. He didn't really expect anyone else to understand. He started to speak, but I stopped him.

"That's okay," I said. "You know? Because it's only the first part of the cycle. You know what's next? Personality reorganization! Sidney, you've got a really positive thing to look forward to."

Sidney sat down on one of the cushions and started to laugh. It doesn't happen often that someone really flashes on the whole cycle like that, and it was a far out thing to see.

"Mr. Beatts," he said. "I don't remotely understand where you're coming from . . ."

"Don't try, man."

"But I think I can flow with it."

STANLEY ELLIN

KINDLY DIG YOUR GRAVE

The story of Madame Lagrue, the most infamously successful dealer in bad art on Butte-Montmartre, and of O'Toole, the undernourished painter, and of Fatima, the vengeful model who loved O'Toole, and of what happened to them, properly begins in Madame Lagrue's gallery on rue Hyacinthe.

It is possible that the worst art in the whole world was displayed on the walls of the Galerie Lagrue.

Madame, of course, did not know this, nor, one must surmise, did her customers. To Madame, every picture on her walls from the leaden landscapes to the tropical moonlights painted on black velvet, from the cunning kittens peeping out of boots to the endless array of circus clowns, some with teardrops

conspicuously gleaming on their cheeks to indicate
the breaking hearts beneath the painted smiles—
every one of these was beautiful.

That was the first reason for her fantastic success
as a dealer in low-priced art—her abominable taste.

The second reason was that long before any of
her competitors, Madame Lagrue had smelled out
the renaissance in faraway America. After the war,
all over that golden land, it seemed, the middle-
aged middle class had developed a furious appetite
for, as Madame's brochure so neatly described it,
*genuine works of art, hand-painted on high quality
canvas by great French artists for reasonable prices.*

So, when the trickle of American interior decora-
tors and department-store buyers became a tide
regularly lapping at the summit of Butte-Montmartre, Madame was ready for it. Before her competitors around the Place du Tertre in the shadow of
Sacré-Coeur knew what was happening, she had
cornered the fattest part of the market, and where
others occasionally sold a picture to a passing tourist, she sold pictures by the dozen and by the gross
to a wholesale clientele.

Then, having created a sellers' market among
those who produced the kittens and clowns, Madame saw to it that she was not made the victim of
any economic law dictating that she pay higher
prices for this merchandise.

Here, her true talent as an art dealer emerged
most brilliantly.

Most of the artists she dealt with were a shabby, spiritless lot of hacks, and, as Madame contentedly observed, their only pressing need was for a little cash in hand every day. Not enough to corrupt them, of course, but barely enough for rent, food, and drink and the materials necessary for creating their pictures.

So where Madame's competitors, lacking her wealth, offered only dreams of glory—they would price your picture at 100 francs and give you half of that if it sold—Madame offered the reality of 20 or 30 francs cash in hand. Or, perhaps, only 10 francs. But it was cash paid on the spot, and it readily bought her first claim on the services of the painters who supplied her stock in trade.

The danger was that since Madame needed the painters as much as the painters needed Madame, it put them in a good bargaining position. It was to solve this problem that she invented a method of dealing with her stable which would have made Torquemada shake his head in admiration.

The painter, work in hand, was required to present himself at her office, a dank and frigid cubbyhole behind the showroom with barely enough room in it for an ancient rolltop desk and swivel chair and an easel on which the painting was placed for Madame's inspection. Madame, hat firmly planted on her head as if to assert her femininity— the hat was like a large black flowerpot worn upside down with a spray of dusty flowers projecting from its crown—would sit like an empress in the swivel chair and study the painting with an expression of distaste, her eyes narrowing and lips compressing as she examined its details. Then on a piece of scrap paper, carefully shielding the paper with her other hand to conceal it, she would jot down a figure.

That was the price the artist had to meet. If he asked a single franc more than the figure on that scrap of paper, he would be turned away on the spot. There was no second chance offered, no opportunity to bargain. He might have started out from his hutch on rue Norvins confident that the property under his arm was worth at least 50 francs this time. Before he was halfway to rue Hyacinthe, the confidence would have dwindled, the asking price fallen to 40 francs or even 30 as the image of Madame Lagrue's craggy features rose before him. By the time he had propped his picture on the easel he was willing to settle for 20 and praying that the figure she was mysteriously noting on her scrap paper wasn't 10.

"*A vous la balle,*" Madame would say, meaning it was his turn to get into the game. "How much?"

Thirty, the painter would think desperately. Every leaf on those trees is painted to perfection. You can almost hear the water of that brook gurgling. This one is worth at least 30. But that sour look on the old miser's face. Maybe she's in no mood for brooks and trees this morning—

"Twenty?" he would say faintly, the sweat cold on his brow.

Madame would hold up the scrap of paper before him to read for himself, and whatever he read there would fill him with helpless rage. If he had asked too little, he could only curse his lack of courage. If too much, it meant no sale, and there was no use raising a hubbub about it. Madame did not tolerate hubbubs, and since she had the massive frame and short temper of a Norman farmhand, one respected her sensibilities in such matters.

No, all one could do was take a rejected picture to Florelle, the dealer down the block, and offer it to him for sale at commission, which meant waiting a long time or forever for any return on it. Or, if Madame bought the picture, take the pittance she offered and head directly to the Café Hyacinthe next door for a few quick ones calculated to settle the nerves. Next to Madame Lagrue herself, it was the Café Hyacinthe that profited most from her method of dealing with her painters.

A vous la balle. It was a bitter jest among the painters in Madame's stable, a greeting they some- times used acidly on one another, the croaking of a bird of ill omen which nightmarishly entered their dreams and could only be muted by the happy thought of someday landing a fist on Madame's bulbous nose.

Of them all, the one who was worst treated by Madame and yet seemed to suffer least under her

oppression was O'Toole, the American painter who
had drifted to Butte-Montmartre long ago in pursuit
of his art. He was at least as shabby and unkempt
and undernourished as the others, but he lived with
a perpetual, gentle smile of intoxication on his lips,
sustained by his love of painting and by the cheapest *marc* the Café Hyacinthe could provide.

Marc is distilled from the grape pulp left in the
barrel after the wine is pressed, and when the wine
happens to be a Romanée-Conti of a good year its
marc makes an excellent drink. The Café
Hyacinthe's *marc*, on the other hand, was carelessly,
sometimes surreptitiously, distilled from the pulp of
unripe grapes going to make the cheapest *vin du
pays*, and it had the taste and impact of grape-
flavored gasoline.

As far as anyone could tell, it provided all the
sustenance O'Toole required, all the vision he
needed to paint an endless succession of pastoral
scenes in the mode of the Barbizon School. The
ingredients of each scene were the same—a pond, a
flowery glen, a small stand of birch trees; but
O'Toole varied their arrangement, sometimes putting the trees on one side of the pond, sometimes on
the other. The warmth of a bottle of *marc* in his
belly, the feel of the brush in his hand, this was all
the bliss O'Toole asked for.

He had had a hard time of it before entering
Madame's stable. During the tourist season each
year he had worked at a stand near the Place du

Tertre doing quick portraits in charcoal—*Likeness Guaranteed or Your Money Back;* but business was never good since, although the likenesses were indisputable, naive and kindly mirror images, the portraits were wholly uninspired. His heart just wasn't in them. Trees and flowery glens and ponds, that was where his heart lay. The discovery that Madame Lagrue was willing to put money in his hand for them was the great discovery of his life. He was her happiest discovery, too. Those pastorals, she soon learned, were much in demand by the Americans. They sold as fast as she could put them on display.

O'Toole was early broken in to Madame's method of doing business. That first terrible experience when he was taught there was no retreat from his overestimate of a picture's value, no chance to quote a second price, so that he had to trudge away, pastoral under his arm unsold, had been enough to break his spirit completely. After that, all he asked was 20 francs for a large picture and 10 for a small one and so established almost a happy relationship with Madame.

The one break in the relationship had been when Florelle, who owned the shop on the other side of the Café Hyacinthe and who was not a bad sort for an art dealer, had finally persuaded him to hand over one of his paintings for sale at commission. The next time O'Toole went to do business with

Madame Lagrue he was dismayed to find her regarding him with outright loathing.

"No sale," she said shortly. "No business. I'm not interested."

O'Toole foggily stared at his picture on the easel, trying to understand what was wrong with it.

"But it's beautiful," he said. "Look at it. Look at those flowers. It took me three days just to do those flowers."

"You're breaking my heart," said Madame. "Ingrate. Traitor. You have another dealer now. Let him buy your obscene flowers."

In the end, O'Toole had to reclaim his picture from Florelle and beg Madame's forgiveness, almost with tears in his eyes. And Madame, contemplating the flow of landscapes which would be coming her way until O'Toole drank himself to death, almost had tears of emotion in her own eyes. The landscapes were bringing her at least 100 francs each, and the thought of 500 to 1000 percent profit on a picture can make any art dealer emotional.

Then Fatima entered the scene.

Fatima was not her name, of course; it was what some wag at the Café Hyacinthe had christened her when she had started to hang around there between sessions of modeling for life classes. She was a small, swarthy Algerian, very plain of feature, but with magnificent, dark, velvety eyes, coal-black hair which hung in a tangle to her waist, and a lush figure. She was also known to have the worst disposition of anyone who frequented the café and, with a few drinks in her, the foulest mouth.

"She's not even eighteen yet," the bartender once observed, listening awestruck as she told off a hapless painter who had sat down uninvited at her table. "Think how she'll sound when she's a fullgrown woman!"

She also had her sentimental side, blubbering unashamedly at sad scenes in the movies, especially those in which lovers were parted or children abused, and had a way of carting stray kittens back to her room on the rue des Saulles until her concierge, no sentimentalist at all, raised a howl about it.

So although it was unexpected, it was not totally mystifying to the patrons of the Café Hyacinthe that Fatima should suddenly demonstrate an interest in O'Toole one rainy day when he stumbled into the café and stood in the doorway dripping cold rainwater on the floor, sneezing his head off, and, no question about it, looking even more forlorn than any of the stray kittens Fatima's concierge objected to.

Fatima was alone at her usual table, sullenly nursing her second Pernod. Her eyes fell on O'Toole, taking him in from head to foot, and a light of interest dawned in them. She crooked a finger.

"Hey, you. Come over here."

It was the first time she had ever invited anyone to her table. O'Toole glanced over his shoulder to see whom she was delivering the invitation to and then pointed to himself.

"Me?"

"Yes, you, stupid. Come here and sit down."

He did. And it was Fatima who not only stood him a bottle of wine but ordered a towel from the bartender so that she could dry his sodden hair. The patrons at the other tables gaped as she toweled away, O'Toole's head bobbing back and forth help-lessly under her ministrations.

"You're a real case, aren't you?" she told O'Toole. "Don't you have brains enough to wear a hat in the rain so you don't go around trying to kill yourself in this stinking weather?"

"A hat?" O'Toole said vaguely.

"Yes, imbecile. That thing one uses to keep his head dry in the rain."

"Oh," said O'Toole. Then he said in timid apol-ogy, "I don't have one."

Everyone in the café watched with stupefaction as Fatima tenderly patted his cheek.

"It's all right, baby," she said. "Someone left one in my room last week. When we get out of here you'll walk me back there and I'll give it to you."

The whole thing came about as abruptly as that. And it was soon clear to the most cynical beholder that Fatima had fallen hopelessly in love with this particular stray cat. She began to bathe regularly, she combed out the tangles in her splendid hair, she showed up at the café wearing dresses recently laundered. And, surest sign of all, the little red welts and the bite marks once bestowed on her neck and shoulders by various overnight acquaintances all faded away.

As for O'Toole, Fatima mothered him passionately. She moved him into her room, lock, stock, and easel; saw to it that he was decently fed and clothed; threatened to slit the throat of the bartender of the Café Hyacinthe if he dared serve her man any more of that poisonous *marc* instead of a drinkable wine; and promised to gut anyone in the café who made the slightest remark about her *grand amour*.

No one there or elsewhere on Butte-Montmartre made any remarks. In fact, with only one exception among them, they found the situation rather touching. The one exception was Madame Lagrue.

It was not merely that paintings of nudes outraged Madame—in her loudly expressed opinion, the Louvre itself would do well to burn its filthy exhibitions of nakedness—but the knowledge that the degraded models for such paintings should be allowed to walk the very streets she walked was enough to turn her stomach. And that one of these degraded, venal types should somehow take possession of a cherished property like O'Toole—!

Madame recognized that the corruption had set in the day O'Toole appeared before her almost unrecognizably dandified. The shabby old suit was the same, but it had been cleaned and patched. The

shoes were still scuffed and torn, but the knotted
pieces of string in them had been replaced by shoe-
laces. The cheeks were shaven for the first time in
memory, and, to Madame's narrowed eyes, they did
not appear quite so hollow as they used to be. All in
all, here was the sad spectacle of a once dedicated
artist being prettified and fattened up like a shoat
for the market, and, no doubt, having the poison of
avarice injected into him by the slut who was doing
all this prettifying and fattening. It was easy to
visualize the way Fatima must be demanding of him
that he ask some preposterous price for this landscape on the easel. Well, Madame grimly decided, if
a showdown had to come, it might as well come
right now.

Madame glanced at the landscape and at O'Toole,
who stood there beaming with admiration at it, then
wrote down on her scrap of paper the usual price of
20 francs.

"Come on," she said tartly, "*à vous la balle*. Name
your price. I'm a busy woman. I don't have all day
for this nonsense."

O'Toole stopped beaming. Just before departing
for the gallery he had been admonished by Fatima
to demand 100 francs for this painting.

"Simpleton," she had said kindly, "you've put a
week's work into this thing. Florelle told me a painting like this was worth at least a hundred francs to
the old witch. You have to stop letting her bleed you

to death. This time if she offers only twenty or thirty, just spit in her ugly face."

"Yes, this time," O'Toole had said bravely.

Now, with Madame's flinty eyes on him, he smiled not so bravely. He opened his mouth to speak, closed it, opened it again.

"Well?" said Madame in a voice of doom.

"Would twenty francs be all right?" said O'Toole.

"Yes," said Madame triumphantly.

It was the first of her many triumphs over Fatima's baleful influence. The greatest triumph, one Madame herself never even knew of, came the time Fatima announced to O'Toole that she would accompany him on his next sales meeting. If he didn't have the guts of a decayed flounder in dealing with his exploiter, at least she, thank God, did. She watched as O'Toole, after giving her a long, troubled look, started to pack his paints together.

"What are you doing, numskull?" she demanded.

"I'm leaving," O'Toole said with a dignity that astonished and alarmed her. "This is no good. A woman shouldn't mix in her husband's business."

"What husband? We're not married, imbecile."

"We're not?"

"No, we're not."

"I'm leaving anyhow," said O'Toole, somewhat confusingly. "I don't want anyone to help me sell my paintings."

It took Fatima a flood of tears and two bottles of *vin rouge* to wheedle him out of his decision, and she never made the same mistake again. It was a lost cause, she saw. All O'Toole wanted besides the pleasure of painting was the pleasure of having a ready cash market for his paintings, and Madame Lagrue, by offering him one, had bought his soul like the devil.

Until she had to face this realization Fatima had merely detested Madame Lagrue. Now she hated her with a devouring hatred. Oh, to have revenge on the evil old woman, some lovely revenge that would make her scream her head off. Many a night after that Fatima happily put herself to sleep with thoughts of revenge circling through her head, most of them having to do with hot irons. And would wake in the morning knowing despondently how futile those happy thoughts were.

Then Nature decided to play a card.

O'Toole was, as is so often the case, one of the last to learn the news. He received it with honest bewilderment.

"You're going to have a baby?" he said, trying to understand this.

"We are going to have a baby," Fatima corrected. "Both of us. It's already on the way. Is that clear?"

"Yes, of course," said O'Toole with becoming sobriety. "A baby."

"That's right. And it means some big changes around here. For one thing, it means we really are getting married now, because my kid's not going to be any miserable, fatherless alley rat. It's going to have a nice little mama and papa, and a nice little house to grow up in. You're not already married, are you?"

"No."

"Well, I'll take my chances on that. And for another thing, we're getting out of Paris. I've had my bellyful of this horrible place, and so have you. We're packing up and going to my home town in Algeria. To Bougie where the kid will get some sunshine. My aunt and uncle own a café there, a nice little place, and they've got no kids of their own, so they'd give anything to have me help them run the joint. You can paint meanwhile."

"A baby," said O'Toole. To Fatima's immense relief he seemed to be rather pleased with the idea. Then his face darkened. "Bougie," he said. "But how will I sell my paintings?"

"You can ship them to your old witch. You think she'll turn down such bargains because they come in the mail?"

O'Toole considered this unhappily. "I'll have to talk to her about it."

"No, I will, whether you like it or not," said Fatima, risking everything on this throw of the dice. "I've got another piece of business to settle with her anyhow."

"What business?"

"Money. We'll need plenty of it to get to Bougie and set up in a house there. And it wouldn't hurt to have a few francs extra put away for the bad times so the kid can always have a pair of shoes when he needs them."

"He?"

"Or she. It's even more expensive with a girl, if it comes to that. Or would you rather have your daughter selling her innocent little body as soon as she's able to walk?"

O'Toole shook his head vigorously at the suggestion. Then he looked wonderingly at the mother-to-be.

"But this money—" he said. "You think Madame Lagrue will give it to us?"

"Yes."

Finally, he had found something on which he could express a firm opinion. "You're crazy," he said.

"Am I?" Fatima retorted. "Well, simpleton, you leave it to me and I'll show you how crazy I am. And get this straight. If you don't let me handle that miserable old hyena my own way, I'll turn you over to the cops for giving me a baby without marrying me, and they'll throw you in jail for twenty years. Nobody does any painting in jail either. He just sits there and rots until he's an old man. Do you understand?"

For the first time O'Toole found himself face to face with a presence even more overwhelming than Madame Lagrue's.

"Yes," he said.

"All right then," said Fatima. "Now get a nice big canvas ready. You're going to paint me a picture."

So it was that a week later, Fatima appeared in the Galerie Lagrue bearing a large painting clumsily wrapped in newspaper. Madame's assistant, a pale, timid girl, tried to bar her from the office and was shoved aside.

Madame was at her desk in the office. At the sight of her visitor, who came bearing what must be an original O'Toole, she quivered with indignation. She aimed a commanding forefinger at the door.

"Out!" she said. "Out! I don't do business with your kind!"

Fatima summed up her answer to this in a single unprintable word. She slammed the office door shut with a backward kick of the foot, hoisted the painting to the easel, and stripped its wrapping from it.

"Is it your business to refuse masterpieces, harpy?" she demanded. "Look at this."

Madame Lagrue looked. Then she looked again, her eyes opening wide in horror.

This painting was larger than any O'Toole had ever offered her before, and it was not the usual landscape. No, this time it was a nude. A ripely curved, full-blown nude with not an inch of her fleshy body left to the imagination. And with Fatima in a tight, highly revealing blouse and skirt standing side by side with the painting, there was no doubt in Madame's shocked mind as to who its model had been. The nude was an uninspired pink and white, not swarthy as Fatima was, but it was without question Fatima's body so painstakingly delineated on the canvas.

But that was only the beginning of the horror, because while it was Fatima from the neck down, it was, abomination of abominations, Madame Lagrue herself from the neck up. Photographically exact, glassy-eyed, the black flowerpot upside down on the head with the dusty flowers sprouting from its crown, the stern face staring at Madame was Madame's own face.

"A masterpiece, eh?" said Fatima sweetly.

Madame made a strangled noise in her throat, then found her voice. "What an insult! What an outrage!"

She came to her feet prepared to rend the outrage to shreds, and suddenly there was a wicked little paring knife gleaming in Fatima's hand. Madame hastily sat down again.

"That's better," Fatima advised her. "Lay one little finger on this picture before you buy it, you old sow, and I'll slice your nose off."

"Buy it?" Madame refused to believe her ears. "Do you really believe I'd buy an obscenity like that?"

"Yes. Because if you don't, Florelle will take it on commission. And he'll be glad to put it right in the middle of his window where everyone on Butte-Montmartre can see it. Then everyone in Paris. Those fancy Americans you do business with will see it, too. They'll all have a chance to see it, blood-sucker, because I'll tell Florelle not to sell it at any price for at least a year. It'll be worth it to him to keep in his window just to draw trade. Think that over. Think it over very carefully. I'm in no rush."

Madame thought it over very carefully for a long time.

"It's blackmail," she said at last in bitter resignation. "Plain blackmail. A shakedown, nothing more or less."

"You've hit the nail right on the head," Fatima said cheerfully.

"What if I submit to this blackmail?" Madame asked warily. "Can I do whatever I wish with this disgusting object?"

"Anything. If you pay its price."

"And what is its price?"

Fatima reached into a pocket and came up with a folded slip of paper which she waved tantalizingly just out of Madame's reach.

"The price is written down here, old lady. Now all you have to do is meet it, and the picture is yours. But remember this. Offer me one solitary franc less than what's written down on this paper, and the deal is off. There's no second chance. You get one turn in this game, that's all. Prove yourself one franc too thrifty, and the picture goes straight to Florelle."

"What kind of talk is that?" Madame demanded

angrily. "A game, she says. I'm willing to do business with this creature, and she talks about games."

"Vulture," retorted Fatima. "Destroyer of helpless artists. Don't you think everyone knows this is the way you do business? *A vous la balle*, eh? Kindly dig your grave, artist, and bury yourself. Isn't that the way it goes? Well, now it's your turn to learn how it feels."

Madame opened her arms wide in piteous appeal. "But how can I possibly know what you intend to rob me of? How can I even guess what it would cost to buy you off?"

"True," admitted Fatima. "Well, I'm softhearted so I'll give you a hint. My man and I are moving to Bougie in Algeria, and we'll need travel money for that. And some decent clothes and a trunk to put them in. And we want to buy a little house there—"

"A house!" said Madame, the blood draining from her face.

"A little house. Nothing much, but it must have electricity. And a motor bicycle to get around on."

Madame Lagrue clasped her hands tightly against her stout bosom and rocked back and forth in the chair. She looked at the nude on the easel and hastily averted her eyes from it.

"Dear God," she whimpered, "what have I done to deserve such treatment?"

"And," said Fatima relentlessly, "a little *pour-boire*, a little money extra to put in the bank like respectable people should. That's what I see in my future, old lady. You've got a good head on your shoulders, so you shouldn't have much trouble adding it all up." She held up the slip of paper. "But make sure your arithmetic is right. Remember, you only get one chance to guess what's written here."

In her rage and frustration Madame found herself groping wildly for elusive figures. Travel money to Algeria, 300 francs. No, 400. No, better make it 500, because rather safe than sorry. Another 500 should certainly buy all the clothes needed for such a pair of ragamuffins. Throw in 100 for a trunk. But a house, even a mud hut, with electricity! Madame groaned aloud. What, in the devil's name, would that cost? Possibly 7000 or 8000 francs. And *pourboire*, the slut had said, and a motor bicycle. There was no use trying to work it all out to the exact franc. The best thing to do was call it a round 10,000.

Ten thousand francs! Madame Lagrue felt as if a cold wind were howling around her, as if she were being buried alive beneath a snowdrift of misery.

"Well?" said Fatima cruelly. "Let's have it. *A vous la balle, madame.*"

"I'll have the law on you," croaked Madame Lagrue. "I'll have the police destroy that scandalous object."

"Save your breath, miser. This is a work of art, and you know as well as I do that nobody destroys a work of art because it might bother someone. Now enough of such nonsense. What's your offer?"

Madame stared at the slip of paper in her tormentor's hand. Oh, for one little look at the figure written on it—

"Ten thousand," she gasped.

The look of contempt on Fatima's face, the curl of that lip, told Madame she had miscalculated after all, she had cut it too fine. She thought of the crowds gathered before Florelle's window staring with obscene delight at the picture; she thought of them gathering before her own window, leering and nudging each other, hoping to get a glimpse of her in her disgrace. She'd never be able to go out on the street again. She'd be driven out of business in a month, a week—

"No, wait!" she cried. "I meant fifteen thousand! Of course, fifteen thousand. I don't know what got into me. It was a slip of the tongue!"

"You said ten thousand."

"I swear it was a mistake! Take fifteen. I insist you take it."

Fatima glanced at her slip of paper. She gnawed her lip, weighing the case in her mind. "All right, I'll be merciful. But I want my money right now."

"I don't have that much in cash here. I'll send the girl to the bank."

"And I want a paper to show that the deal is strictly on the level."

"Yes, of course. I'll make it out for you while we're waiting."

The pale, timid assistant must have run like a

rabbit. She was back in almost no time with an envelope stuffed full of banknotes which she handed to Madame Lagrue through the partly opened door of the office. Tears trickled down Madame's cheeks as she gave the money to Fatima.

"This is my life's blood," Madame said. "You've drained me dry, criminal."

"Liar, you've made a million from your poor painters," Fatima retorted. "It's time at least one of them was paid what you owe him."

As she left, she crumpled the slip of paper in her hand and carelessly tossed it to the floor.

"You don't have to see us off at the plane," she said in farewell. "Just stay here and enjoy your picture."

No sooner had the office door slammed behind her than Madame snatched up the crumpled paper from the floor and opened it with trembling fingers. Her eyes, as she saw the figure written on it in a large childish hand, almost bulged from her head.

Twenty francs!

Madame Lagrue wildly pounded her fists on the desk and screamed and screamed until the frightened assistant had to throw water in her face to quiet her.

GREGORY MCDONALD

THE NINE BEST MOVIES

The first time her house was broken into, she called the police.

"What has actually been taken, Mrs. Reagan?"

"Well, nothing. It's all rather mystifying. When I arrived home, I saw the house had been broken into. The coffee table had been pushed over there. That chair had been moved. The ashtrays were full. I called you immediately. Then I went around the house. My jewelry is in the dresser. My mink is in the closet. Two hundred dollars I leave in an old handbag in the closet is still there. Nothing is missing."

"Nothing?"

"Well, a Sara Lee chocolate cake I was defrosting. And I think two Hershey bars, although I might

have eaten them myself." The officer had written
nothing in his notebook. "Really, I feel rather
foolish."

"Do you live alone, Mrs. Reagan?"

"Yes. I'm a widow. I write on movies for *The
Press*, you know, so I'm away a lot."

"I see."

The officer looked through the open doorway to
the typewriter and masses of fresh and used paper
on the dining table. Back issues of *The Press* were
scattered everywhere. It had been so long since she
had given anyone dinner.

His partner came through from the kitchen.

"Absolutely no sign of forced entry," he said.
"Back door, front door, even the windows upstairs."

"The cellar door." Her voice seemed loud. "I
mean, doors. There's never been a hasp on the
bulkhead. And there's never been a way of locking
the cellar door in the kitchen."

She stepped toward the kitchen but the officers
moved toward the front door and they all stopped.

"Well, yes, ma'am. We'll file a report, even though
nothing was taken. And we'll keep a better watch
on your house while you're away. You might get
one of those electric light timers."

"I have one," she said. "It costs a fortune to run."

"And you might get someone to put a lock on
your bulkhead."

"Yes," she said.

"Good night."

After her warm tub she sat on the divan in her robe and slippers with a glass of mash and water. The television did not work. She had pulled every window shade in the house. She felt so vulnerable.

She had moved the coffee table back. In the ash-tray were three kinds of cigarettes, a white filtered, a brown filtered, and a filterless. So there had proba-bly been at least three people in the house. Going around the room, she collected all the ashes into one tray. There were more bits of unburnt tobacco in the ashtray than one would expect. She sniffed the mess and discovered it wasn't all tobacco.

As she had to write for both the daily and Sunday newspapers, Irene Reagan was apt to make her overnight trips away at the end of the week. During the season she would be away one or two nights every week, or more, if she then went away for the weekend.

After her next trip, the house was in the same disarray. The coffee table and chair had been shoved away from the center of the room. Some bologna, bread, and a six-pack of beer had been consumed. Four beer cans were in the kitchen wastebasket, one was on the coffee table, and one was upstairs in the bathroom. The mayonnaise jar had been left open on the kitchen table. She threw it away.

Simple figuring had decided her against putting locks on the cellar doors. Getting a workman to do it for her would cost more than the worth of anything that had been stolen. It was an old house in the suburbs, and she knew perfectly well if people wanted to get in they could get in easily enough. Then she would have to pay for smashed glass.

Before going away next time, she typed out a note and left it on the coffee table. THE LEAST YOU MIGHT DO IS CLEAN UP YOUR OWN MESS.

It was the day after she returned, when she settled at the dining room table to work out a Sunday feature story, that she found the answer in her typewriter. WHY DON'T YOU GET YOUR TELEVISION FIXED?

She flew to Stockton, California, Wednesday night, where Stanley Kramer was filming and spent the weekend with her friend, Carol Masterson, who had retired with her husband to Palm Springs.

Sunday night the house was in its usual mess. Irene was bone weary, suffering more than usual from jet lag, horrified by the writing week she had before her, so she took her glass of mash upstairs to drink while her tub was running. Her bed was unmade. So was the bed in the guest room. Her vexation diminished in the hot tub after the mash. Her originally stiff attitudes toward teenage sex had been dissipated by too many bad movies.

Nevertheless, before her next trip she left this note in her typewriter: AT LEAST YOU COULD CHANGE THE SHEETS.

She giggled at the answer: INTO WHAT?

After her next trip the television was missing and, saying to herself, this is getting serious, this is intolerable, somebody needed some money for something, for some more pot, she called the police.

"I could never get the UHF to work anyway," she said. "And a black band had been appearing down two inches from the top."

"A color set?"

"Gracious, no. Just an old Zenith. First one made, I think."

"Has anything else been taken?"

"Some Oreos."

"What?"

"Some Oreos. They're a cookie."

The policeman wasn't writing anything in his book again.

"I never did get the cellar doors fixed," she said, hoping to see the policeman remember. One was the same who had come before.

"Well, we'll report your television is missing," he said. "And you should get those doors fixed."

"I know teenagers need a place to go." Her hand was against the edge of the open door. "But really, this is ridiculous."

After her next trip, the television was back. Fixed.

Without pulling the shades, she curled up on the divan and enjoyed three glasses of mash while she watched Allan Trustman's *They Call Me Mister Tibbs!* That night she slept beautifully.

Before going away again she made a double-layered chocolate cake and left it in the washed cake pan on the kitchen table. She hadn't made a cake in years. She left a half gallon of milk in the refrigerator. Upon her return, one generous piece of cake and a glass of milk had been left for her. She had cake and milk instead of her usual drink before turning in.

Thereafter she left a six-pack of beer, fresh bread, and some sandwich meat before she went away each time. It was rather fun figuring out what her guests liked and remembering to shop for them. And she cleaned the house and frequently had to change the sheets for them.

On a Wednesday night there was a reception in town for some Canadian filmmakers, a dressy affair. Reaching into the back of her closet for a pair of formal shoes, plastic sticking out of her gardening boots caught her eye. It was a good-sized bag of marijuana, sealed with masking tape. Inside the bag also was something that looked like an eyebrow tweezer.

She sat on the edge of her bed with the bag in her hands to think a moment. I am in possession of marijuana. I have been in possession of marijuana. My left gardening boot has been used as a stash. I have summoned the police twice to go all over my house while I have had marijuana stashed in my left gardening boot.

Chuckling to herself, she put the marijuana into the right gardening shoe, and just for fun moved it about eighteen inches toward the back of the closet under a hanging clothes storage bag. They would find it, but they would have to look. She imagined the moment of panic when they discovered their pot gone. At least they would know thereafter that she voluntarily was in possession of marijuana. Clever kids. Anyone looking at her yard would know she was a lousy and infrequent gardener.

"Teenagers do need a place to go," she said to herself.

In preparation for her next trip, she left two six-packs of beer (she understood from some movie or other that smoking pot makes one thirsty), some cold cuts, potato salad. She also left a letter from her son in Chicago casually tossed on the coffee table. He wrote infrequently, and the letter said nothing. But she did want them to know there was someone who related to her somewhat.

After cleaning the house after her next trip, starting to work at the dining room table, she found a note stuck in her typewriter.

DEAR MRS. REAGAN: WE ALL READ YOUR MOVIE REVIEWS AND WE THINK YOU'RE AN AWFUL MOVIE REVIEWER SO WE DECIDED WE'D HELP YOU OUT. WE KNEW YOU'D BE DOING YOUR AWFUL "TEN BEST MOVIES OF THE YEAR" ARTICLE SOON SO WE THOUGHT WE'D GIVE YOU OUR TEN BEST MOVIES OF THE YEAR.

The list followed.

They were a little early, but they were right: she

would be writing that piece within a week or two. She might as well do it right then.

"I usually offer my humble opinion as to what were the ten best films of the year," she wrote, "but this year I offer instead a list compiled by a group of teenagers who frequently visit my house. Only I cannot allow one movie to stand on the list of the best of this year again as the movie *2001* was originally released in 1968. So here goes with the list of the nine best movies of the year . . . "

Returning from the trip following publication of the nine-best piece, she almost wept. The house looked as though it had never been disturbed. The coffee table and chair were where she liked them. The ashtrays were empty. The beds were made. She felt immensely relieved to find the cigarette ashes and empty beer cans in the kitchen wastebasket.

But it was after the next trip she found the following note in her typewriter: SANDRA GOT ACCEPTED AT HARVARD.

Immediately she sat down and typed out, using the same piece of paper: OH, DARLINGS, I'M SO PLEASED. . . .

HENRY SLESAR

I DO NOT LIKE THEE, DR. FELDMAN

Dr. Horace Feldman arrived at Ponchawee Manor with every expectation of being liked. The boy who handled his luggage liked him and admired the Feldman Mercedes. The lady in Registration beamed the moment the Feldman paunch touched the front desk. The resort manager, Mr. Glassmacher, shook the Feldman hand, but gently, gently, in consideration of those surgeon fingers. A gratifying entrance, but no surprise to Dr. Feldman, a man accustomed to admiration, liking and respect.

There were two married couples and a widow lady at his assigned table in the dining room. Her name was Mrs. Shear, and 60 isn't so old when an unmarried 50-ish doctor with a healthy round face and a cute mustache breaks bread beside you. "So you're a surgeon, Dr. Feldman?" she said coyly and nudged Stanley, the busboy, in the ribs. "Stanley, tell the cook he don't have to carve the roast beef tonight, we got an expert." Dr. Feldman chuckled and ingested his soup. Before the coffee, he admitted to being a specialist, performing the only operation of its kind on the iliolumbar artery, on cases that would otherwise prove fatal.

"Fortunately," he said, "not many people need the operation; but when they do, they come to me."

Mrs. Shear clapped her hands and crowed: "A monopoly!" But money, the monopolist said, didn't matter; half his patients were charity cases. At this assurance, everyone liked Dr. Feldman even more. Not only was he a life-giving surgeon with gold fingers, he was a human being with a golden heart. And a fine gin-rummy player. Later that evening, he won $14 from Mrs. Shear, her friend Mrs. Elkins and two men, both named Harry. Everybody liked him. It looked like a good week at Ponchawee Manor.

The next day, another new arrival was placed at the table (it quickly became known as the Feldman table) and the doctor was surprised to get a grunt instead of a how-do-you-do, when he introduced himself. The man's name was Moritzer. He was in his late 40s, sallow, thin and unhappy-looking. A bad choice for the Feldman table, the others agreed, sitting on the porch after lunch.

Dr. Feldman submitted a defense. "Don't judge so quick," he said. "Moritzer may not be feeling so well. Moritzer may have business troubles. Give Moritzer a chance."

He gave Moritzer a chance at the rec hall. "Well, what's your pleasure?" he asked. "Gin rummy I'm tired of. Like to shoot some pinochle? You play Ping-Pong? How about pool?"

"No, thanks," Moritzer said coldly. "I came here to rest, not play games."

"You live in the city?" Dr. Feldman said.

"Yeah, so what?"

"Nothing, nothing," the doctor said. "I don't think I heard your first name. Mine is Horace. I always hated that name. They used to call me Horse. That wasn't so bad when I was a little runt, but then I put on a few pounds," he chuckled and patted his solid midsection. "What's yours?"

"My name is Moritzer," the man said.

Later that evening, Dr. Feldman was playing checkers, and winning. Then he looked up and saw Moritzer in a rocker, regarding him with eyes that could curdle sour cream. The Feldman hand shook and he lost the game.

He was going into his room (the Feldman suite) when he saw Moritzer coming down the hall, slapping his thigh with a rolled-up evening newspaper.

"Good night, Mr. Moritzer," he said.

Moritzer didn't answer. Didn't even *answer*.

Dr. Feldman had a little trouble getting to sleep that night and he blamed the newcomer. Moritzer meant nothing to him, of course; just a sourpuss; but Dr. Feldman was troubled. Could it be that Moritzer actually didn't like him?

That possibility, remote as it seemed, persisted at

dinner the next day. Moritzer was not merely surly; he was selectively surly. He actually spoke a few words to the married couples. He actually answered Mrs. Shear's questions about his marital status (he was married, but his wife didn't like the country). But to Dr. Feldman: not a word.

A lesser man might have been comforted by indignation or contented with indifference. Not Dr. Feldman. To the Feldman psyche, Moritzer's attitude was a challenge.

After dinner, the doctor said: "Come for a walk, Moritzer."

"I hate walks," Moritzer said.

"Good for digestion. Doctor's orders."

To his surprise, Moritzer grunted and agreed. They walked down the main road and into the narrow wooded road that circled Ponchawee like a lasso. By mutual assent, they were silent. Here and there, the path narrowed and grew rocky. Now and then, one or the other would lose his footing.

"Careful, careful," Dr. Feldman said when Moritzer stumbled against him.

"Careful yourself," Moritzer said unpleasantly. A few steps later, he tripped and almost knocked the doctor over. The Feldman temper was held, but then it happened a third and a fourth time.

"Hey, careless," he said, with a forced smile. "Watch where you're shoving."

When they got back to the Manor, the doctor was taking pine needles out of his sleeve, looking ruffled. Mrs. Shear asked him how the walk was. Fine, he said.

The next day, only moderately daunted, he invited Moritzer to mixed doubles on the badminton court. The team of Moritzer-Elkins *vs.* Feldman-Shear. A top attraction. Actually, Moritzer turned out to be a gloomy but quick-moving opponent, and Mrs. Elkins wasn't bad, either. Feldman-Shear lost badly. Then the ladies suggested a variation: the boys against the girls. That would have been all right, but twice, *twice* Moritzer struck the doctor on the back of the head with his racket. Once was an accident, Dr. Feldman told himself. But twice?

That afternoon, Dr. Feldman went for his first dip in the Ponchawee pool, setting an example for the timid. An hour later, one of the married couples, Mrs. Elkins, Mrs. Shear and even Moritzer turned up in swimsuits. It developed that Moritzer was a nifty swimmer. Unlike the doctor, who required water wings, he wore swim fins and a face mask and spent a lot of time under the water. The result was a lot of giggling from the women and some naughty remarks. Then a funny thing happened. The surgeon was doing the Feldman crawl, a dignified movement, slow but effective, when he felt a hand close about his ankle. It *had* to be a hand, he reasoned; there wasn't any aquatic life in the Ponchawee swimming pool. And the hand seemed intent upon pulling Dr. Feldman beneath the surface. At first, he reacted good-naturedly, calling out merrily, "Hey, cut it out down there!"; but when his nose filled up with chlorinated water, he wasn't so amused. "Blub, glub!" Dr. Feldman cried and kicked out with his other foot to strike a shoulder bone or something equally hard—a face mask, maybe? The hand let go and the doctor, panting, paddled to the pool's edge.

That night, the Feldman sleep was disturbed by a dream of drowning. It was no wonder, then, that he hesitated at Moritzer's very first overture of friendship at breakfast.

"Come for a row," he said.

"A row," Dr. Feldman said, thoughts of water.

"On the lake."

"The lake," Dr. Feldman said and then decided he was being silly. "Fine idea! Look, let's invite the women."

"Phooey," Moritzer said. "I'm a married man. Enough is enough. You want to go for a row, OK. If not, OK."

"OK," Dr. Feldman said.

They went down to the boathouse and took out the soundest-looking rowboat. It was a beautiful day. The lake was glassy, except for a ripple here and there that indicated the presence of a fish warming itself near the surface. When Dr. Feldman learned that tackle was also available, he suddenly enthused. Moritzer didn't fish, but he liked to row. The labors were divided. Feldman: fishing. Moritzer: rowing.

The boat skimmed the water smoothly under Moritzer's easy oar stroke. The doctor was willing to fish in the middle of the lake, but Moritzer wanted to round the bend and head for a more distant shore. After a while, they couldn't see the pink roof of Ponchawee Manor anymore.

For half an hour, Moritzer napped in the rowboat and Dr. Feldman fished. But nothing nibbled on the Feldman line and Moritzer started getting restless. He sat up on the other side of the craft and regarded the doctor with folded arms and baleful eyes. Then he began a slow rocking from side to side.

"Shush," Dr. Feldman said. "You'll scare the fish."

"What fish?" Moritzer said.

Soon the rocking became more violent.

"Moritzer," the doctor said, "what are you doing?" Moritzer didn't answer. He just stared and rocked. "Moritzer, are you crazy? You keep this up, you'll turn the boat over."

"So?"

"So what do you want us to do, drown?"

"What's the matter, Feldman?" Moritzer said nastily. "You didn't bring your water wings?"

"A joke is a joke," the doctor said frostily. "Let's go back already."

Unbelievably, Moritzer stood up. He planted his feet on both sides of the vessel and rocked so hard that the boat began shipping water.

Dr. Feldman looked incredulously at the water stains on his white-duck trousers and cried out: "Moritzer, I believe you're a crazy man!"

"Yeah, so learn how to swim, Feldman," Moritzer

said, and the doctor began to realize that maybe
Moritzer, sullen Moritzer, didn't just *dislike* him,
maybe Moritzer really *hated* him, maybe Moritzer
wanted him *dead*.

"*Moritzer!*" the doctor screamed, as he felt himself losing his balance. He grabbed the side of the
boat for support and found himself clutching one of
the oars. He slipped it out of the lock and tried to
use it as a balancing pole. This made Moritzer
laugh. He sounded like one of those fiends in the
old movies, and Dr. Feldman was terrified. He
didn't have to *think* about hitting Moritzer with the
oar, he just did it. He caught Moritzer broadside on
his left ear, and Moritzer went sleepy-looking and
toppled over the side and into the water with a
mighty splash. The boat was capsized a moment
later and, for a grim five seconds, Dr. Feldman
thought he was underneath it. But, no—there was
daylight and, gasping, sputtering, making all kinds
of heaving noises, he managed to cling to the bottom. He didn't worry about looking for Moritzer; he
was too busy holding on and yelling. It wouldn't
have mattered, anyway, because Moritzer was
already drowned and dead.

The rest of Dr. Feldman's visit to Ponchawee
Manor was less enjoyable. There were policemen
and a local reporter and plenty of clucking tongues
in the dining room, and the doctor was content with
the official version of the story that soon circulated
around the resort and found its way onto the police
blotter. It was an accident, of course (and maybe,

Dr. Feldman thought wishfully, maybe that's all it was), and Moritzer's drowning was explained by the blow on the head he sustained when the boat capsized. Dr. Feldman thought it was permissible not to mention the business with the oar, just as he didn't mention Moritzer's deliberate rocking. Fair was fair. But he wasn't sorry to climb behind the wheel of his Mercedes and put Ponchawee Manor behind him. In fact, he was actually happy to return to the office Monday morning and see the unlovely but not unwelcome face of Hilda, his nurse.

"Well, doctor?" she said. "Did you have a good time?"

"Not bad, not bad," Dr. Feldman said. "Only, there was a little accident—"

"You weren't hurt?" Hilda asked with quick concern.

"No, no," Dr. Feldman said. "But some poor man got drowned. Otherwise, I had a wonderful time. Now," he said, rubbing his surgeon's hands together in anticipation of saving yet another life, "who's our first patient this week?"

"It's a Mrs. Moritzer," Hilda said.

EDWARD D. HOCH

THE MOST DANGEROUS MAN

The professor glanced up from the desk where a new treatise on the binomial therorem lay open before him. His ears had detected a noise upon the landing—not loud, but enough to sharpen his senses. When it was repeated, he rose from the chair and walked across the room to the bolted door.

"Who is it?" he asked.

"Dwiggins, Professor! Open the door!"

The bolt was pulled back and the professor turned up the gas-flame a bit higher. "You arrived sooner than I had expected. Did all go well?"

Dwiggins was a slender man with black bushy hair and side-whiskers. His special value was his innate ability to assume the guise of a bumbling tradesman. The professor had known and used him many times in the past, always with success.

"It was perfect, Professor," reported Dwiggins. "I arranged a meeting with Archibald Andrews and told him of my needs. He agreed quite readily when I revealed the sum of money I was willing to pay."

"Capital, Dwiggins!" The professor drew a small note-book from his pocket and made a check mark. Then, with the tip of the pencil running down a list of names, he said, "We will have a final meeting to-morrow evening. Make certain everyone is in attendance."

"Right you are, Professor!"

When he was alone once more, the tall pale man hurried to the window and watched the progress of Dwiggins along the opposite curb. His deeply sunken eyes scanned the alleyways, searching for a police-agent who might be following the bushy-haired man, but he saw no one. Thus far, nothing had happened to endanger his master plan.

The flickering gas-flames cast an uncertain glow over the five men who gathered in the professor's quarters the following evening. They were a mixed lot, drawn from various walks of life, but each had been chosen carefully for his special skills and accomplishments. Seated next to Dwiggins was Coxe, the notorious bank robber, and by his side was Quinn, an expert with a knife who proudly boasted for having been a police suspect in their search for Jack the Ripper only two years earlier. Moran, the former army colonel, was present too, along with Jenkins, a street ruffian especially adept in the handling of horses.

"Now, now," said the professor, peering and blinking at the men before him. "We must get to the business at hand."

"Will it be to-morrow?" asked Coxe.

The professor nodded. "To-morrow, the twenty-third of January, the City and Suburban Bank will make its regular Friday morning delivery of money to its branches. A two-horse van will enter the alleyway off Farringdon Street shortly after nine o'clock to-morrow morning, and proceed to the rear entrance of the bank. The flat of one Archibald Andrews overlooks this alley, and our Mr. Dwiggins has been most successful in luring said Andrews away from his flat for the entire morning. Tell us how it was accomplished, Dwiggins."

The bushy-haired man was quick to oblige. "I approached Andrews yesterday afternoon. Knowing him to be temporarily unemployed, I presented myself as a spice merchant with expectations of setting up a small shop in Oxford Street. I offered to pay him ten pounds if he would spend Friday morning visiting a list of shops and noting the prices charged for a variety of spices. He is to begin at Covent Garden Market promptly at eight, which should keep him far enough from his rooms in Farringdon Street."

"Tut, tut!" said the professor, shaking his head sadly. "I fear that Archibald Andrews will learn more about the price of spices than he really needs to know. Coxe, you should have no trouble with the door to his lodgings. You and Quinn will enter the rooms at precisely half-past eight, and station yourselves at the windows overlooking the alley. When the two-horse van arrives for the money, you will open the windows and prepare to jump. As I explained earlier, there is no manner in which the robbery can be executed while the money is being loaded. The armed guards will be on the alert for trouble. And once it leaves the alley to move through the crowded London streets it will once again be safe from our hands. The one weak link in the chain occurs at the precise instant the van is locked and starts out of the alley. The armed guards will have entered a carriage to travel ahead of the van, and the van itself will be travelling so slowly that you two can easily drop into it from Mr. Andrews's second-storey windows."

"Excuse me, Professor," said Coxe. "I understand all that, but what will the two guards in the carriage do when they realise we have intercepted the van?"

The professor merely smiled, blinking his puckered eyes. "Everything is attended to. Jenkins here will be near at hand, in the guise of a hansom driver. At the proper moment his horse will appear to go out of control, and will carry the hansom cab between the guards' carriage and the van. Quinn will kill the driver of the van, and you will turn it in the opposite direction on Farringdon Street, away from the carriage. If the guards are able to get clear of the hansom and pursue you, Moran will be waiting with his air-gun."

"Where will you be?" asked Quinn.

"Dwiggins and I will be waiting close by. Once you are on your way, we will follow." He turned and took a cut-glass decanter from the sideboard. "Now, gentlemen, I suggest a bit of wine to toast the success of our endeavour on the morrow."

When Archibald Andrews left the doorway of his lodgings just before eight o'clock the following morning, Dwiggins and the professor were watching from across the street. It was a raw, blustery January morning, and the professor had turned up the collar of his greatcoat against the sharpness of the wind.

"Running like clockwork," Dwiggins commented as he watched Andrews go off down the street.

"Good, good!" The professor slipped a watch from his inner pocket and snapped open the lid. "Coxe and Quinn should be starting out now."

They waited, watching the movement of shopgirls and clerks along the busy street. Then, at half-past the hour, the professor saw his two confederates enter the street door to Archibald Andrews's lodgings. Dwiggins returned from his rounds to report. "Coxe and Quinn are in the flat, Professor. I saw them by the windows."

"And Moran?"

"He has just arrived and stationed himself across the street from the alley. The air-gun is hidden in his walking-stick."

"Jenkins?"

"His hansom is parked near-by."

The professor nodded. All was well.

At six minutes after nine o'clock, the two-horse van appeared and turned into the alley. A carriage drew up behind it and discharged two uniformed guards. The professor's face was oscillating slowly from side to side, in a curiously reptilian fashion, as he watched.

They waited while the minutes ticked by and the professor's sharp eyes scanned the passers-by for any sign of trouble. There seemed nothing unusual until—

"Dwiggins!"

"What is it, Professor?"

"That man hurrying through the crowd across the street—is it Archibald Andrews, returning so soon to his lodgings?"

"Bloody right it is!"

"Come on, we must stop him."

They crossed the street quickly, and Dwiggins called out, "Here, now! I hired you to do a job for me!"

Archibald Andrews stopped in his tracks, looking from one to the other. "I—I—"

"Speak up, man!" urged Dwiggins. "This is my partner in the spice shop. Do you have the prices for us?"

"No, sir," muttered Andrews. "That is, you see, it seemed like a great deal of money for you to pay. I mentioned it to a friend of mine last evening—a physician who rooms with a consulting detective of sorts. He suggested something odd might be afoot."

"Quickly," snarled the professor. "If he comes here—"

But already there was movement in the alley. The guards' carriage had moved away, and the two-horse van was starting out with its precious cargo. As the professor watched, he saw Coxe and Quinn throw back the shutters and drop through the windows onto the roof of the van.

In the same instant there came the sound of police whistles, and suddenly the van seemed alive with uniformed bobbies. Coxe and Quinn were seized by a dozen strong arms.

"Quickly!" the professor told Dwiggins. "We must make our escape!"

"What about the others?"

But it was too late for them. Jenkins, abandoning his hansom for flight on foot, was in the clasp of a tall, sharp-featured man whose long white fingers seemed to clutch like steel.

"It is too late for them," the professor decided.

"We can only hope that Moran was able to make good his escape."

"How did the police discover our plans so quickly?"

"That man is a devil!—that tall one who had Jenkins in his grip! As soon as he discovered that Andrews's lodgings overlooked the alley by the bank, he must have known we were luring the man away for a number of hours while we used his flat to reach the money-van."

"All that because I offered Andrews ten pounds?" Dwiggins followed the professor down a side street, away from the bustle of the crowds. "Who is this man that outwitted us?"

"His name is Sherlock Holmes," answered Professor Moriarty. "He is the most dangerous man in London."

JEFFREY BUSH

THE LAST MEETING OF THE BUTLERS CLUB

The last meeting of the Butlers Club can hardly be said to have been a complete success. Meat loaf with ketchup—the only dish that agreed with both the members' elderly stomachs and their less elderly teeth—can scarcely be called the *pièce de résistance* of a gourmet dinner. Nor can the sudden and practically simultaneous deaths of all those who ate it, some 20 minutes later, be seen—except, perhaps, from the most judicious perspective—as a fitting climax.

Still, the festivities, while they lasted, were decidedly high-spirited. At about five o'clock—for the members adhered to the dinner hour that they had observed during their professional careers—the first guest arrived at the secluded but unobtrusively elegant section of London in which the Butlers Club has (or, one must now regretfully say, had) its permanent headquarters.

Assisted on one side by Morgan, the Club's resident Steward, and grasping the iron rail on his other side with a gnarled hand, the first arrival made his way up the front steps, through the hall, and into the lounge, where he undid the heavy overcoat he had bundled himself into on that cold Friday evening in January and sank happily into the most comfortable of the five leather chairs in one corner of the large oak-paneled room—chairs discreetly redisposed to conceal the absence of a sixth, which had, alas, been recently removed. (There was a time, years ago, when the Club's membership numbered in the dozens, nay, in the scores.)

Soon afterward came the next guest. By five-thirty all five members had tottered joyfully in, apart from old Phillips, who made his entrance in a wheelchair, and old Murgatroyd, whose habitual expression was one of alert anger. For the next half hour the gurgle of unblended Scotch whiskey filled the air—in the matter of the Club's liquid provisions, no expense was spared—together with the crackle of a small fire and the sound of squeaky but animated voices discoursing enthusiastically on their latest ailments.

At exactly six o'clock the figure of Morgan, the thin, deferential, middle-aged Steward—*young*

Morgan, he was known as—appeared to announce that dinner was ready.

Nor does he deny that it was *his* dinner. He readily admits that he cooked it in the basement kitchen, he carried it upstairs, and he served it. He was, after all, the only servant on the premises—the Butlers Club's butler.

By a succession of gravity-defying movements old Stanley, the President, levered himself from his chair. Old Murgatroyd followed, looking about him with an angry scowl to see whether anyone was challenging his second, or Vice-Presidential, place. After him old Phillips went into motion, restraining himself out of a sense of decorum, since he was naturally the swiftest, by reason of his wheelchair. And one by one the five surviving members of the Butlers Club trooped and stumbled to their last repast.

"Very tasty," old Phillips remarked, and shoveled in another mouthful.

It was generally agreed that old Phillips, being on wheels, was permitted to eat the main course with a spoon. There had never been an agreement, however, that old Murgatroyd was. He had simply begun to, angrily, three years ago.

"Tangier than last year," old Simpson agreed in a quavering voice.

The section of meat loaf he had been conveying to his mouth slipped off his trembling fork and fell with a plop into his ketchup. Poor old Simpson, someone had said earlier in a loud and carrying tone—probably old Phillips, a keen-eyed observer—looked shakier than ever. Undeterred, old Simpson commenced new maneuvers with his fork.

By this time the slender and retiring hand of young Morgan had filled the wineglasses from a bottle with a label almost as faded and venerable as the diners.

"Gentlemen," the President announced at the head of the table, "a toast."

There was a general clatter of silverware being lowered—or, in the case of poor old Simpson, dropped—and glasses being raised.

"To the old days!"

"To the old days!" repeated a surprisingly strong chorus of reedy voices.

Swallows were swallowed, glasses were set down, lips were smacked.

"Good stuff," old Phillips stated from his wheelchair.

"Very good," old Simpson echoed waveringly, still absorbed in the process of putting down his glass.

"Yours?" inquired old Bates, halfway down the table, looking up at the President. Thanks to an unfortunate malady with a Latin name, old Bates was unable to hold his head more than two or three inches above his plate, from which position, although it was convenient for eating, he had to peer up and sideways at whomever he was addressing.

"Bequeathed to me," the President replied, "by my old master." And for an instant an extra bit of light seemed to dance in his sparkling old eyes.

"To his old master!" old Phillips said, raising his glass.

"To *all* our old masters," old Murgatroyd amended, in a tone that would have been taken as bad-tempered from anyone else.

More swallows. Glasses put down again. And for a moment, for the space of an old heartbeat, an odd sense of something in the air—something like a roar of laughter—about to explode. But kept back, with difficulty, as the five members returned to their dinner. And young Morgan began deftly to refill their glasses.

"Don't suppose," old Bates observed, peering up in his sideways fashion, "they ever thought we'd be enjoying ourselves like this."

"Never *dreamed* it," old Murgatroyd corrected.

"Poor fellows," old Phillips said. And there was another beat of bursting silence, of barely suppressed hilarity, as each pair of ancient eyes looked into another pair, moved on, and gleefully met the next.

Had someone tittered? Old Murgatroyd, the Club crosspatch? Quickly, before anything unseemly could take place at the dinner table, the President

looked up and down its shimmering white length.
"More meat loaf?" he asked.

Old Bates, his chin down to his chest, struggled to
his feet. "Tell young—young what's-his-name"—
for it is a curious fact that the members of the
Butlers Club were seldom able to remember the
name of their own butler, though he had been with
them for 20 years—"to bring brandy and cigars to
the lounge."

Which was done. And after young Morgan had
been casually dismissed, the members found themselves, agreeably full, reinstalled in their leather
chairs, except for old Phillips, who retained his
private, movable accommodations—though a
leather chair was always ready for him, in case he
should undergo a miraculous recovery—puffing
thick cigars and sipping antique brandy. Plus, for
the President and old Murgatroyd, decaffeinated
coffee.

"Good meeting," old Simpson declared.

"Excellent," old Phillips agreed.

"So far," old Murgatroyd added, visibly mel-
lowed, with only an undertone of his customary
rage.

"Any business?" old Bates asked, his cigar held at
a careful distance from his face, which was bobbing
close to his lap.

"Not that I know of," the President answered.

"What about the finances?" old Murgatroyd
demanded, irascibility boiling nearer to the surface.

"In splendid shape," said old Phillips, who was the Treasurer.

"Investments?"

"Doing well," old Phillips replied. "Sold a block of property in the West End."

"Why?"

"Advised to. By our brokers."

"What did we buy?"

"Saudi Arabia."

"What?"

"Large tract in Saudi Arabia."

"Why did we do that?"

"Said to have oil in it. Seemed like a good idea."

"Hmm," old Murgatroyd said, temporarily appeased.

There was a satisfied pause.

"Remarkable what can be done," old Bates said, looking about the handsome room with a sly, sideways grin, like an ancient Richard III, "with a few modest bequests. A pair of cuff links here. A hundred pounds there. An old family painting. An acre or two of the family land. A few shares of the family business. Put together, by humble fellows like us, and allowed to grow."

"Astonishing," old Phillips said.

"Sobering," the President said, gazing at the end of his cigar.

"And so simple, really," old Bates said.

This time the silence was almost solemn.

"Not many fellows like us left," old Murgatroyd observed.

"Young what's-his-name, I suppose," old Phillips said, waving his cigar toward the door through which young Morgan had departed.

"But not like *us*."

"Think he should have a raise?" old Bates said.

"Who?" old Murgatroyd said.

"Young Morgan?"

"What for? Hasn't complained, has he?"

"Odd chap," the President remarked. "Never complains about anything."

"What's he got to complain about?" old Murgatroyd asked. "He's the Steward, isn't he?"

Old Simpson lifted a trembling finger. "Cold toilet."

"Eh?" the President said.

"Toilet," old Simpson explained. "Cold."

"Cold?"

"When you sit down on it."

"What are you doing sitting down on young Morgan's toilet?"

"He doesn't mean young Morgan's toilet," old Phillips said. "He means ours."

"Electrically heated," old Simpson said.

"He means," old Phillips said, "he wants an electrically heated toilet seat."

"I'll see what I can do," the President promised.

"Why shouldn't a fellow have an electrically heated toilet seat?" old Bates said. "In his own club?

After he's gone through what we've gone through?"
And in his single visible eye, peering up and
askance, was a gleam of triumphant mirth.

"I'll say," old Phillips exclaimed. And blew out
an explosive puff of smoke.

"Ha!" old Murgatroyd ejaculated.

It was the President, drawing on his cigar, his lips
on either side of it elevated in what those who knew
him could tell was Presidential levity—it was he
who was the first to give way. "I shall never forget—" he began, and the others understood that the
time had come, at last, to indulge themselves in the
greatest pleasure of their annual meetings. An hour
or two of reminiscences. "I shall never forget the
look on my mistress' face, as she stood in the dock
in Old Bailey, and the Judge handed down his
sentence."

"What was it?" old Phillips asked, settling back in
his wheelchair.

"Twenty years, poor lady. Though it was later
much reduced, for good behavior."

"No, no," old Phillips said. "What was the look
on her face?"

"Incredulity," the President said, with a faraway
look on his own round pink face. "That such a thing
should be happening to her."

"But it was," old Phillips said helpfully.

"Yes." The President drew again on his cigar. He
tapped the ash from it. "Perhaps you have forgotten
the details." No one there had forgotten the details,

except old Simpson. They had heard the details annually for more than 30 years, but they were glad to hear the details once more, provided their own turns would come soon. "On the night in question, that resulted in my lady's tragic appearance in the dock six months later, my master was sleeping in the summerhouse."

"Why?" old Simpson asked.

"Why what?"

"Why was he sleeping in the summerhouse? Wasn't it winter time?"

"I forget," the President said. "There was some adequate explanation given at the time. It was the sort of thing often done by the landed gentry of that period. In any event," he went on, a trifle testily, "it was not relevant to the case."

"Oh."

"What *was* relevant, however, was that at some time during the night it began to snow."

"Snow," old Simpson repeated attentively.

"The next morning he was discovered. Dead. By the parlormaid who had gone to change the sheets."

"Change the sheets?"

"The sheets of his bed," the President explained, a shade impatiently, "were changed daily. Whether he slept in the summerhouse or the main house."

"Ah."

"There were two sets of footprints in the snow."

"Two sets of footprints." Old Simpson enumerated them on his first two fingers.

"One set leading to the summerhouse, and the other back to the main house."

"What about hers?"

"Hers?"

"The parlormaid's?"

The President drew a deep breath.

"Hers do not count."

"Oh."

"The parlormaid is of no importance."

"Ah."

"The important fact is—*there was only one pair of feet large enough to have made those two sets of footprints.*"

With no change of expression on his round imperturbable countenance, the President regarded the polished black toe of one of his size-12 shoes.

Old Simpson leaned forward. "What happened?"

"The local bobby was about to take me off to the station house when a gentleman whom my master had invited to spend the weekend arrived in a small sports car. He was, he said in an aristocratic voice, an amateur detective who had had some success in America with apparently insoluble cases of this sort."

"Insoluble?"

"Precisely the question raised by the local bobby, who then outlined the evidence of the footprints in the snow. But the gentleman glanced at me and inquired whether I was concerned about getting my feet wet."

"Were you?"

"Certainly, I told him, but in the flurry of being arrested that morning I had been unable to find my galoshes. Whereupon he turned to the bobby and suggested in an amused, sardonic manner that it might be a mistake to arrest the most obvious suspect."

"Why?"

"Cases of this sort, the gentleman implied, were never obvious. It took a superior brain like his to solve a classic puzzle like this. He referred to the bobby as 'old thing.' Persuaded him to wait until Monday, pointing out that communications in this part of England were already paralyzed by the two-inch snowfall. And after a day and a half of whistling snatches of operatic music and quoting bits of Latin and looking at the feet of the neighbors, the local clergy, and the tramps of the vicinity, the gentleman announced that he'd found the guilty party."

"And it wasn't you?"

"All I stood to gain, he explained, was a small pension. And a few bottles from the wine cellar. It was the person who'd been overlooked from the beginning—my mistress."

"But how could she have made those footprints?"

"By borrowing my galoshes."

"Whew." Old Simpson sat back, as relieved at the

outcome as he had been the first time he had heard it, 33 years ago.

Old Bates shook his bobbing head in wonder. "Amazing piece of reasoning."

"Did she ever give them back?" old Simpson asked. "Your galoshes, I mean?"

"Claimed she never had them. Lucky for me the gentleman had been invited."

"Who was he?"

"Vance was his name," the President said gravely. "Philo Vance."

There was a respectful pause.

"Reminds me of the chap who solved my case," old Phillips said from his wheelchair. "Thorndyke. Dr. Thorndyke."

"Ah, yes," the President said, relighting his cigar. Now that he had finished his own narrative, he could afford to be a polite interlocutor.

"Scientific investigation was his line," old Phillips went on in his rich, bass voice, like a large invalided bullfrog. He took a sip of brandy. "No personality to speak of. Practically no first name. But a wonderful mind. Thorough. Methodical. Always picking up things, putting them in little envelopes, and looking at them through a microscope."

"And he played a part in your case?"

"Fortunately. For me." Old Phillips pointed dramatically at the floor. He made up for the immobility of his lower half by oratorical gestures.

"There," he said vibrantly, "was my master's

body. Shot, in the library, with the fatal revolver
lying beside him on the Oriental rug. And there"—
he pointed in the opposite direction, which happened to be the ceiling—"was a house full of
guests. Including his first wife, his daughter by his
second wife, his aunt by his mother's third marriage, his niece by his sister's first marriage to his
fourth cousin, and his son-in-law, a nervous chain
smoker."

"A whole crowd of suspects, eh?"

"Too many for Scotland Yard. Call in Dr.
Thorndyke, they agreed. And the first thing he said,
when he made his inconspicuous appearance, was,
'We can eliminate the servants.' "

"Reassuring."

"I don't mind telling you I was glad to hear it.
'They are only receiving a few insignificant
bequests,' he said, 'in the form of old family portraits.' Then he said he was going to examine the
revolver in his laboratory, to see if there were any
fingerprints." Old Phillips paused rhetorically.
"Sure enough, there were."

"Whose?" asked the President, who knew quite
well.

"Mine."

"A disturbing development."

"Bit of a facer for Dr. Thorndyke, too. 'Have you
recently mailed a bulky parcel?' he asked me. 'As a
matter of fact,' I answered, 'yesterday I posted my
master's stuffed rhinoceros head to a dry-cleaning

firm.' 'Was it possible to wrap it adequately with string?' 'No,' I said, 'it wasn't. I had to use a roll of sticky tape.' 'How did you know that?' the Scotland Yard man asked, perplexed. 'I fear,' Dr. Thorndyke replied, 'that this case is less simple than it may have at first appeared.'

"The industrious fellow spent the next three days with his fingerprint powder and magnifying glass before he turned to the son-in-law and said quietly, 'When did you ask Phillips the butler to light your cigarette with your silver cigarette lighter?' Baffled looks on the faces of the other guests, assembled in the library. On mine, as well. 'Why,' stammered the son-in-law, 'I may have done so on the day I sprained my wrist while getting out of the bathtub, making it inconvenient for me to operate my cigarette lighter myself, a few hours before my father-in-law was shot.' Bewildered gasps.

" 'If indeed you did suffer such an improbable accident,' Dr. Thorndyke said. 'If, instead, it was not part of your carefully conceived plan to gain control of the family fortune by shooting your father-in-law with a revolver to which you then *transferred Phillips the butler's fingerprints from your cigarette lighter by means of adhesive package-sealing tape.'* "

Old Simpson whistled.

Old Bates drew an admiring breath.

"Astounding bit of deduction," the President said.

Old Phillips, sitting back in his wheelchair,

observed with gratification the effect he had created in his audience.

"Almost as good as my case," old Murgatroyd said irritably.

"Almost?" Old Phillips raised his eyebrows good-naturedly.

But old Murgatroyd was too engrossed to notice. "Imagine," he began, clenching his bony hands on the arms of his leather chair, "my master and me, alone in the billiard room. With the door open. And with the sworn testimony of three independent witnesses, guests at the house party, that no one else had passed through that door."

"Locked room, as it were, eh?" old Phillips said agreeably. "But with an open door?"

"Imagine the sound of an agitated cry. Of a body falling. Imagine, immediately thereafter, my master's twin brother, recently returned from a visit to Australia to take charge of the family's flourishing umbrella-stand factory, rushing into the room to discover my master dead on the floor, of a gaping wound. While I stood over him clasping the hilt of the angular medieval knife that ordinarily hung on the wall."

Old Bates peered up and sideways.

"Good heavens," old Phillips said.

Old Murgatroyd nodded grimly. "A difficult situation."

Old Simpson, who had been sitting with his

mouth open, closed it. And opened it again. ''What did you say?''

''On the spur of the moment I could not think of anything suitable to say.''

Old Phillips clicked his tongue. ''Open-and-shut case.''

''So it appeared. Until Lord Peter entered it.''

''*The* Lord Peter?''

''The Lord Peter.'' Old Murgatroyd's bony face softened. ''Charming man. Made one conscious that one belonged to the lower orders, but that one *liked* it. 'Oh, no,' he said to the Inspector, when he'd assembled us all in the billiard room to reconstruct the crime, 'it's not the butler.' 'Not the butler, Wimsey?' the Inspector said disbelievingly. 'Standing over the body? With the knife in his hand?' 'I fancy you'll find,' Lord Peter said, in his kind, boyish, impulsive way, 'that young what's-his-name—'

'' 'Murgatroyd?' the Inspector supplied. 'That young Murgatroyd,' Lord Peter went on, 'who, by the way, is only gettin' a modest annuity and two or three acres of the family estate, was simply pullin' the knife out of the wound to see what could be done for his master.' To which I gratefully agreed. And my master's attractive daughter, whom I'd known since she was a baby, gave my hand a little squeeze.

''The Inspector looked dumbfounded. 'But this *is* the knife that made the wound?' 'Oh, yes,' Lord Peter said, 'no doubt about that.' 'And nothing went through that door, according to three independent witnesses who were sitting within six feet of it?' 'Nothing,' Lord Peter said, 'human.' The Inspector turned pale. 'Good God. Something—supernatural?' 'More interestin' than that,' Lord Peter said, and turned carelessly to face my master's twin brother.

" 'Delightful summer we've been havin', isn't it?' 'Unusually pleasant,' the twin brother agreed, at a loss. 'Not for someone, though, who's borrowed heavily in the City,' Lord Peter went on remorselessly, 'on the strength of an increased demand for umbrella stands.' 'But—' the twin brother began. 'I suppose as soon as you saw this curiously shaped knife you knew it could be used in a rather special way.' 'Special way?' 'Thrown around a corner— through an open door—past three independent witnesses—as *an Australian boomerang.*'

"The others exclaimed with mingled horror and relief, while the twin brother stood there speechless, and the Inspector clapped the handcuffs on his wrists. 'But how could you be so sure,' the Inspector said, 'that it wasn't Murgatroyd?' 'Who?' Lord Peter asked, with that endearing forgetfulness of his. 'Murgatroyd,' the Inspector said, 'the butler.' 'Oh, the butler. It always looks as if it's the butler.' There was a mischievous twinkle in Lord Peter's eye. 'It looks as if it *must* be the butler, on Friday, when the body's discovered. But by Sunday night it always turns out it isn't.'

"Then he stopped, and grew serious. 'Wouldn't be fair, really, would it, if it was? If you couldn't count on spendin' the weekend explorin' the case? And analyzin' the problem? And usin' your intelligence? And findin' someone else?' "

This time no one spoke. Old Simpson stared into the dying fire. The President drew on what was left of his cigar, looked at it, and stubbed it out. Old Phillips sighed.

"Reggie Fortune was the one who solved my case," old Simpson said tremulously. "Plump chap. Relied on his intuition. Kept saying, 'Oh, my aunt!' "

"They brought Max Carrados into my case," old Bates said wistfully. "Blind fellow. Used his other phenomenally developed senses."

"Remember Trent?" the President asked. "Father Brown? Inspector French? Albert Campion, obscurely related to royalty?" He surveyed the room, as if searching in the deepening shadows for a sixth chair, and a seventh, and an eighth, which were no longer there. "All the others?"

One nostalgic old voice followed another.

"Working out their timetables?"

"Drawing their diagrams of the bedrooms?"

"Interrogating the guests?"

"Hypothesizing?"

"Investigating?"

"Reasoning?"

"Never resting until they'd proved it wasn't the butler?"

"The obvious suspect?"

"But someone else?"

"Until they'd discarded the simple solution?"

"And thought up another?"

"That was *really complicated?*"

Old Phillips snorted. Old Simpson emitted a quavering guffaw. Old Bates, his head bobbing faster, began to chuckle. The President allowed his round cherubic face to break into a very slow, very broad smile.

"Silly asses," he said.

Old Murgatroyd was the only one who sat with a preoccupied expression on his bony, ill-natured features. "I say," he remarked peevishly, "do any of you chaps think there was something odd about the meat loaf?

Three-quarters of an hour later, young Morgan testified that he found, when he entered the room to ask if anything more was required of him, that the last five members of the Butlers Club had gone to their rewards. To judge from their attitudes, they had passed their final moments endeavoring to reach either the bell or—for both were located on the same sideboard—the brandy bottle.

Whatever contribution they could have made to our knowledge of the wave of weekend country-house murders that swept over England in the '20's and '30's has gone with them. The mystifying circumstances of their own deaths, however, may soon be solved. Young Morgan was the first to come under suspicion, when it was discovered that a quart of liquid drain cleaner had been mixed into the meat loaf. But that explanation was quickly dismissed.

Scotland Yard, with the help of a number of amateur experts, is now working on the theory that the drain cleaner was frozen into tiny ice pellets, which, during one of his absences from the kitchen, were shot through the bars of the basement window, perhaps by a South American blowpipe, and which then melted, leaving no trace of the ingenious murder method, while the empty bottle of drain cleaner was tossed into the kitchen waste receptacle to confuse the authorities.

A distant cousin of old Bates, they point out, has just returned from a trip to the Amazon. And young Morgan stands to gain nothing from the evening's extraordinary events, according to the Club's constitution, but a few wine bottles, cuff links, paintings, stock shares, and real-estate holdings.

CHARLES R. McCONNELL

SIDNEY, SETH AND S.A.M.

In January seventy-year-old Sidney Currier talked
back to his brother, Seth, two years his senior, for
the first time in their lives. Talking back, actually
arguing with Seth and even insulting him, turned
out to be exactly what Sidney needed. His
"damnfool impertinence," as Seth called it,
encouraged Sidney to believe that he may have
found something that had eluded him for years.
Because of this discovery Sidney was not at all
surprised to find himself thinking about killing
Seth.

January was but the beginning. By July Sidney
truly believed it would be possible for him to leave
this life with the upper hand over his domineering

older brother. He, Sidney, would have the last word. The last word ever.

All their lives Seth had scolded Sidney, had berated and demeaned him, and, when they were boys, had often beaten him. And Seth had always had the last word, always fired the parting shot, whether in response to one of Sidney's whimpered protests or simply as punctuation to Sidney's silent suffering. Sidney spent much of his life cringing, knowing that each encounter with Seth was lost before it was begun. Sidney thought of many brave and clever things to say only long after the opportunities to speak them had passed.

Before July trickled into August Sidney had grown certain that his redemption lay in the last word. He would have the final word by assisting fate to an extent sufficient to assure that Seth expired wordlessly. Sidney did not believe that he was actually contemplating murder; Seth, bedridden and in continually worsening pain, was well on the way toward the inevitable. Sidney preferred to think of it as simply giving fate a slight nudge at the right time.

In the way of preparation Sidney had concocted a potent substitute for one of his brother's numerous prescriptions. Seth would appear to have overdosed on his own medication. It remained only for Sidney to decide the proper time.

Most of the world cared little about Seth and Sidney Currier. Some people deferred to Seth as they will cater to anyone who possesses millions of dollars, but none sought his company. Seth's corporations ran reasonably well without him; he permitted—rather, demanded—brief visits by his top managers once each week.

Sidney still operated the little pharmacy founded decades earlier by their father. He felt he could not afford to retire. A small man with a pinched, persimmon face, he worked every day, carrying an air of gloom and suffering through all he did. Seth, with his wealth, was considered eccentric. Sidney was simply odd. As a rule, people avoided them both.

Early in September Seth seemed to rally. He was able to spend an hour at a time out of his bed and in the reclining chair in his room. Sidney thought he might have missed his chance, but his fears were without foundation. Seth's good turn faded rapidly, and soon he was again confined to his bed and his mountain of feather pillows.

It was raining the Monday in mid-September when Sidney paid his second-last visit to his brother. Seth's manservant, the stone-faced, ageless Bardolf, stepped into the bedroom at precisely the appointed 1:00 PM and announced as he did every day, "Mr. Sidney has arrived, sir."

Sidney felt his daily wave of resentment toward the cool, efficient Bardolf. The way the servant announced Sidney he may as well have said *Master* Sidney—never *Mr. Currier*, or *sir*, as Seth was

addressed. Always distantly polite—for Bardolf
there seemed no other way than the polite way—
but always with a sense of second-class regard. And
the gap between first and second class seemed great
indeed.

Bardolf backed out of the room and closed the
door. Seth trailed a limp finger along a row of
buttons on a panel on his overbed tray, and three
television screens went blank.

Wordlessly, as every day, Seth extended his right
hand with palm cupped as though catching rain-
drops. Sidney shuffled to a medicine-laden night-
stand and from several amber containers assembled
a collection of four different colored pills and two
matching capsules which he gave to Seth. Seth took
the medicine with a small paper cup of water Sidney placed in his other hand. Then Seth leaned his
head back against his mound of pillows and closed
his eyes.

Sidney waited in silence, as he waited every day,
for perhaps a minute. Seth opened his eyes and
smiled—or smirked?—at Sidney.

"Good day, brother," Seth chirped, his crackling
voice belying his cadaverous appearance. "Come
for your daily repartee? You've gotten kind of
mouthy lately, heh?"

Sidney looked toward the full wall of electronic
equipment. Four televisions, two video recorders, a
video-disc player, an elaborate stereo system, two
video game sets, and occupying a whole corner of

the large room, a home computer and word processor. A tape recorder and a dozen or so cassettes lay on the bed within Seth's reach.

Sidney waggled a finger at the largest of the television receivers and said, "That wasn't here yesterday."

"That's because it was delivered this morning, dummy."

The insult slid past Sidney. The names he had been called all his life now had little or no effect on him. He simply said, "Waste of money, Seth. Can't watch them all at once."

Sidney shook his head. His permanent frown deepened and he added, "Never will understand the way you accumulate this electronic junk. Or why you're constantly playing with it."

"Because I love it," Seth snapped. "If it's electronic, I want it. I love it, and it's how I've always kept up with the competition." He stretched a thin arm toward the newest television. "Pretty good set. If I was the man I used to be twenty years ago I would've had the damned thing apart by noon. And would've found a way to build it better and cheaper."

"Waste, waste," clucked Sidney.

Seth chuckled. "Been in the kitchen in the last couple years? Microwaves, food processors, convection ovens, you name it. Too bad Bardolf's so old-fashioned about cooking."

Seth continued, "All-new security system for the house, too."

"Third one, as I recall," said Sidney.

"Fourth. With pressure-sensitive alarms in the floors of the library and study."

"Useless."

"No, dummy. Fun. Electronics has been good to me. It's made me a fortune. Several fortunes. And I love every last electronic gadget ever made and every one yet to be made. I've come a long way and gotten a lot of fun out of father's little bequest."

Sidney snorted. "You needn't remind me again that *you* got father's money."

"Can it, Sidney. Don't be a wimp."

Sidney's eyebrows rose a fraction. He didn't know what *wimp* meant, but he was sure it wasn't a compliment.

"Sure, I got the money," said Seth, "and you got the pharmacy. We split father's estate down the middle according to his will. The pharmacy student and the young engineer. What better way? But I took my share and hustled it into an electronics empire while you spent nearly half a century spinning your wheels in the same little drugstore."

"Father didn't like me. You saw to that. You've been nasty to me all of our lives, Seth."

"Hogwash. It's just that you've been a jerk most of our lives. No opinion. No backbone. No guts. Damn it, Sidney, nobody can walk on you unless you *let* them do it. I'm a walker, brother, and you've always been a rug."

Sidney squared his meager shoulders and settled into the straight chair beside Seth's bed. "That's over," he said. "Now I see you for what you are, nothing but a rich, selfish man with a big mouth. And a cruel streak."

Seth's sunken eyes sparkled and he chirped, "Damn, Sid, you're all right! Another seventy years and I might even get to *like* you. You don't know how good it's been to have you visit since you started speaking up."

"Fine time for both of us," Sidney muttered. "You're a physical wreck and—"

Seth interrupted, "—and about to cash in at any moment, and you're an emotional wreck twisted by seventy years of cringing." He grinned and added, "Not to mention being a wimp."

Sidney's anger broke through. "Damn! Always the barb. Always the insult. Seth, if it's the last thing I do on this earth I'm going to —"

Sidney caught himself starting to speak of his carefully nurtured daydream. The last word. To walk away from Seth for the final time having delivered the final word. It need not be special, original, or particularly vicious. It simply had to be last.

"Going to pop a blood vessel. That's what you're going to do."

"Seth, you are . . . insufferable!"

"Come on, brother, you can do better than that."

"You're cruel—"

"You already said that. Come on, be original."

" . . . and . . . and arrogant, and selfish—"

"Ditto for selfish."

"—and just plain nasty."

Seth was making a strange sound that Sidney, after a few seconds' observation, interpreted as laughter. For fully a minute Seth laughed, his frail body quivering and heavy veins dancing beneath the parched skin of his neck. "Oooo! Oooo! You . . . are . . . *funny*! Damn, you're funny. I love it!"

"Seth, for heaven's sake I—"

A muted buzz sounded from the control panel near Seth's right hand. With visible effort Seth brought himself under control and twice pressed a single button. He said to Sidney, "You'll have to leave early. Now. I'm expecting a visitor and I believe he's here. But please come as usual tomorrow. And sharpen your tongue some more."

Sidney rose from the chair. There was a soft knock at the door. Sidney paused near the door and said, "Very well, Seth. I'll return tomorrow—should I think you're worth the time and trouble."

The door opened as Sidney was about to touch the knob. Bardolf was there, and behind him was a lean, silver-haired man wearing a business suit and carrying a briefcase. Past Sidney—or perhaps even through Sidney—Bardolf announced, "The gentleman from the S.A.M. Company, sir."

"Come in," said Seth.

As the door closed behind Sidney, Seth called out, "Are you sure you remember the way out, Sidney?"

The door latched under Bardolf's firm hand. It was all Sidney could do to hide his rage from the servant. Seth had gotten in the last word again, and if he should be so thoughtless as to die within the coming twenty-three and a half hours Sidney would have lost everything.

By the time they reached the front door Sidney had his anger under control. He felt resentment for the visitor for cutting short his visit with Seth, and he asked Bardolf, "Who is that man with my brother?"

"A Mr. Raven of the S.A.M. Company."

"What is the S.A.M. Company?"

"Beyond being Mr. Currier's most recent corporate acquisition I really don't know, Mr. Sidney. Space-age something, I believe. Electronics, no doubt."

"Hmmpf! It figures. More electronic toys. Or more profits he'll never spend."

"Good day, Mr. Sidney."

No new work was waiting for Sidney when he returned to the pharmacy. Most of his customers were regulars of many years, and most of them were aware of the midday closing of the prescription counter while Sidney visited Seth. Sidney's young clerk, Elliott, was busily unpacking and storing the week's wholesale drug order when Sidney resumed his place at the rear of the little store.

Between filling the few prescriptions that trickled in that afternoon, Sidney pondered the future. Each time his mind was free to pursue the matter of Seth he came back around, by whatever route, to the same thought, and each time he arrived there an unpleasant tingle of anxiety crawled up into his rib cage: *Seth could die at any moment, and if he does I will have lost.*

A dozen times that afternoon Sidney examined the small plastic vial he had prepared. Two instant-dissolving capsules. Seth's regular prescription, but forty to fifty times the usual concentration. They would begin to work within a minute of passing the tongue. Muscle paralysis, constriction of the throat, the beginnings of death by suffocation as swift and certain as a cobra bite. Seth would be able to neither speak nor breathe, but for a moment he would see and hear. Especially *hear*, which was important to Sidney.

"Mr. Currier?"

Sidney jumped. The vial clattered on the counter. His heart racing, he covered the vial with a trembling hand. Yanked from his reveries, he looked up into the face of young Elliott the clerk.

"Sorry to startle you, sir. All locked up. Anything else before I go?"

"Hm?" Sidney shook his head. "No, you may go."

But as Elliott said good evening and turned to leave, something Sidney had been curious about since his visit with Seth came forward begging to be known. Perhaps Elliott would know.

Sidney began, "Ah . . . a moment, please, Elliott."

With elevated brows the youth turned back to face his employer. Sidney took little note of the young man's puzzlement, for Sidney would not have been aware that he had never before addressed Elliott by any designation other than *young man* (as he did occasionally) or *you, boy* (as he did most of the time).

"Yes, Mr. Currier? There *is* something?"

Sidney began, "Just a point of information for an old man somewhat out of touch with certain things. You are young and presumably familiar with . . . ah . . . the language of the day. Tell me, Elliott, what is a . . . *wimp*?"

Sidney was flattered by Elliott's willingness, even eagerness, to converse. They talked for nearly half an hour.

It proceeded exactly as Sidney had mentally rehearsed it dozens if not hundreds of times. He was so familiar with every move that he was barely conscious of actually doing rather than just think-ing. It was, as Sidney would later reflect, perfect. A triumph. Completely as planned, except for his final words which had been chosen only that morning.

The visit began as usual. But as Seth, emaciated

hand extended, waited for his medicine, Sidney tipped the container of capsules without removing any and then added the other pills to the two special capsules already in his hand.

Then the cup of water. Seth took his medicine and closed his eyes.

Before stepping back from the bed Sidney silently pocketed Seth's nearly full prescription container and replaced it with an identical, but empty, container. He then went to the foot of the bed and waited for Seth to open his eyes.

A minute, a minute and a quarter. Then a minute and a half. A touch of apprehension. Was it too much? A miscalculation that . . . ?

Seth's eyes opened. Wide. His jaw tensed but did not move.

Sidney smiled. "Do you feel well, brother? Where's your smirk? Your insults?"

Seth's old eyes, fixed on Sidney, grew glazed and round. One gnarled hand clawed air and the other clutched at bed covers. A half dozen tape cassettes clattered against each other as they tumbled to the carpeted floor. Seth's back arched; his meager chest rose.

It would be over in seconds. Sidney backed toward the door as he spoke. "You are finished, Seth. Your greed and your cruelty avail you nothing. I have won. You have been truly nothing, Seth. You are, in fact"— Sidney would be eternally grateful to young Elliott— "a perfect *nerd*!"

The upraised hand dropped and Seth sank deep into his pillows. His eyes remained open, still oriented toward Sidney, but something was missing from them.

Sidney let himself out of the room and out of the house. There was a spring to his step and he hummed all the way back to the pharmacy.

Sidney minded not at all that Seth was buried on a colorless, unseasonably cold day. He thought it a fitting farewell for a cold man.

There was but one seat at graveside. Sidney occupied that single seat. Bardolf, the silent servant, stood directly behind Sidney.

Across the open grave and plain casket stood a new monument, a smooth obelisk of dark stone some five feet tall. Halfway up its height Seth's name and years of birth and death were chiseled. Just above the name was a small plate some four inches square, but Sidney's aging sight denied him its details.

The lean, somber funeral director read a few standard words of farewell over the casket. Then the funeral director and his young carbon-copy assistant cranked the casket into the grave.

The funeral director and assistant and the six pallbearers, the managers of Seth's six largest enterprises, withdrew from the site. Sidney stirred to rise but Bardolf's gentle grip on his shoulders told him he must not move.

Bardolf's right hand moved and Sidney glanced to the side to see the hand disappear and reappear holding a dark object about the size and shape of a cigarette package. There was a muted click followed by a soft whirring sound that Seth could not place.

"Good day, brother. Welcome to my funeral."

Sidney's jaw dropped. He could find no words, no coherent thought. Perhaps ten seconds passed before he realized that the voice came from the tombstone. With this knowledge he was now able to recognize the indistinct plate on the stone for what it was—the grille of a small speaker.

"Seth! It's Seth!"

The voice intoned cheerfully, "How do you like my S.A.M.? That's *space-age monument*, the original solar-powered, solid-state talking tombstone. *I* liked it so much I bought the company."

Sidney moaned.

"Been planning this for months. Got hundreds of hours of tapes, Sidney old boob, and you're going to visit me here and listen for an hour a day for the rest of your life. You're going to because your inheritance of three-quarters of my considerable estate is conditional on your doing so."

"I won't," Sidney barked at the monument. "I won't, you can't make me, I don't want your money. You're dead, Seth, you're dead! I refuse your money!"

Sidney squirmed in the chair through a brief silence before the tape resumed: "Get any little outbursts out of your system? Any stupid threats like perhaps refusing my money? In case you have any such ridiculous ideas, I've left the remainder of my estate to the loyal Bardolf—on the condition that he assure your presence here every day."

The pressure on Sidney's shoulders increased ever so slightly.

Sidney pressed his knuckles to his teeth and moaned his misery toward the open grave. A tear escaped from the corner of each eye. "All lost. It was perfect and it's all lost. My precious last word, my—"

A squeeze on one shoulder cut short Sidney's words. Bardolf said, "Quiet, please, Mr. Sidney, your brother is speaking."

Sidney lifted his chin. The tape was running: "—preliminaries are out of the way, let's get into the first of many, many visits to come. Sid, old dummy, I can tell you why you've always been the way you are. It goes way back to . . . "

Sidney wept as the voice rattled on.

FRED S. TOBEY

YOU DRIVE, DEAR

When Charity Tisdale told her husband she wanted to learn to drive an automobile, she knew he would insist on teaching her himself, not because of any solicitude as to the quality of the instruction but to save money. George Tisdale was a miser, a skinflint, a thoroughgoing penny-pincher. At least that is what Charity would have said had you asked her.

And he did teach her himself, or at least he tried. It was not easy, for Charity was careless, witless and empty-headed. At least, that is what George would have told you had you asked him. He often told Charity without being asked.

From this you will gather that the first bloom of love and affection had departed from the Tisdale marriage, and something resembling antipathy had taken its place. However, though each was often heard to say, in response to some word or action, "I could kill you for that," it is not likely that either had any conscious intention of doing away with the other.

But one night opportunity flaunted itself so brazenly before Charity that she could not overlook it. They had been to a party in a neighboring town, and George had drunk more than he could conveniently hold. In the old days, knowing he would have to drive home, George would have been more cautious; but lately he had fallen into the habit of letting down the bars of restraint, knowing that Charity, now at long last a licensed driver, would take the wheel if necessary. Tonight it was very necessary. When they left their friends' house, George could barely walk, let alone drive.

On the winding road through the South Hills, George was dismayed suddenly to find that he was going to be sick. He demanded of his wife that she pull over to the side of the road immediately.

The area was undergoing scenic improvements, and the usual wooden barrier at the far side of a small field where the terrain dropped away to the valley below had been replaced temporarily by sawhorses with flashing lights. However, there was plenty of space and George's urgency seemed to be great, so Charity quickly pulled the car off the road and brought the sedan to a stop.

Bright moonlight illuminated the valley with a lovely radiance that was completely lost on George as he steadied himself with one hand on a sawhorse. Nature's beauties were lost, too, upon his wife, for as she watched George with distaste it occurred to her quite suddenly that only a little push would be needed to send him careening into the void. Quite on impulse she left the car and administered the push, making it an extra good one just in case. With an exclamation of astonishment, George went over the edge and disappeared.

Not a headlight was to be seen in either direction, so, since there seemed to be no reason to hurry, Charity thought she might as well see just what had become of George. Cautiously, because of her fear of high places, she went to the edge and peered over. Yes, there he was, and his position on the moonlit rocks far below left no doubt of the success of her act. There had not been a tuft or a twig to slow his tumbling descent through two hundred feet of clear mountain air. Since death must have been instantaneous, Charity did not even feel squeamish about letting her eyes rest on the distant body while she recalled, for a long, long moment, just a few of the innumerable reasons why her husband had so richly deserved his fate.

Charity's sister Sarah poured a little more tea for Detective-Sergeant Rourke. She had been having her tea when he arrived.

"Well," she said, "you can keep on asking questions as long as you like and I'll do the best I can to answer them, because you're a police officer, but I just don't see what earthly help you're going to get from anything I can tell you."

"There's the matter of trying to get at a motive somehow," said the sergeant patiently. "Find a motive and you've solved a case, more often than not. We're still not satisfied on the motive and we've been hoping something you would tell us might help."

"They were fighting all the time. I told you that."

"Yes. True enough. But that doesn't quite seem to explain everything, as I think you can see. What did they usually quarrel about?"

"Oh, it didn't make any difference to them; they could fight about one thing just as easy as another. It was something different every day and twice on Sundays. If she said it was going to rain, he'd say it was going to be fine, and off they'd go again, hammer and tongs."

"It's a puzzling case," said Seargeant Rourke. "I'd be glad enough to call it a traffic accident or a double suicide and consider it closed, if I could just figure how the pair of them could have got out of the car while it was falling through the air. It hit the rocks farther down than they did, there's no doubt about that."

The seargeant rose and picked up his hat.

"Well, I'll be running along now," said he, "but I

may be back again, so if you think of anything, keep it in mind."

"Your mentioning the car reminds me," said Sarah, "that was one of the things they liked best to shout about, and the windows never rattled so loud as when they were in the middle of some argument over him teaching her to drive. I recall now, the very morning it happened they were screaming their heads off at each other over some little thing she couldn't seem to learn, or at least that was what he said."

"And what was it she couldn't learn, do you remember?" said Sergeant Rourke, walking toward the door.

"Why, it seems to me—yes, it started when he said anybody who thought she was as good a driver as *she* thought she was, ought to be able to remember to put the hand break on *once* in awhile when she parked the car."

JEFFREY BUSH

THE PROBLEM OF LI T'ANG

I had a problem. I had sixteen midterm papers from my course on Chinese painting, the first papers from the first course I'd ever taught, and one of them was brilliant.

I'd spent the evening discovering from the first seven or eight of the other papers I'd reluctantly looked into that "Chinese painting is beautiful because—" and "The reason I like Chinese painting is—" The opening paragraph of this one stopped me in my tracks. I woke up, sat forward, began again, and proceeded with difficulty, through the rest of it.

It could hardly be called easy reading. But important pieces of Chinese painting criticism seldom are. And that's what this was.

It almost certainly ought to be published.

It almost certainly *had* been published.

And there, of course, was the problem. In my first term of teaching, I realized with a growing sense of exhilaration, I almost certainly had a case of plagiarism.

I got up from the sunken coffee table in the living room of my apartment and mounted the wrought iron steps to the built-in, free-form bar. I'd gone to a certain amount of trouble to find quarters with the sort of conveniences I was accustomed to. This overpriced and somewhat overdramatic penthouse had become available when its tenant had been revealed as the central figure in a series of elaborate criminal activities. I made myself a vodka and tonic, sat down on one of his bar stools, and rested my feet on his curved rail. For the first time I began to feel at home there.

I looked out his picture window at his view of midwestern city lights at one o'clock in the morning and considered what to do.

A tricky business. Made trickier by my mysterious position in the art department.

I had a year's appointment at what I shall describe simply as a large state university. It was a decidedly shaky appointment. All that anyone had known about me when I arrived was that James Harris, recent Ph.D., even more recent victim of a slipped disk (the unfortunate young man had bent over to pick a slender scholarly volume out of a bottom shelf and had been unable to stand up), had been hired, without an interview, to teach Far Eastern art this fall on the basis of three letters of recommendation, the book he had made out of his thesis, and his reputation. Since then, thanks to my bad manners, my having changed apartments, and my general inscrutability, no one had found out much more.

Tall, bony, rude, youthful Dr. Harris was on trial. Very much on trial. If he wanted to have his appointment renewed for another year, he was going to have to come through in the clutch.

Good. I felt the familiar symptoms. The blood moving toward the brain. My fingers tapping on my vodka and tonic. One foot jiggling on the rail.

This was the kind of thing I enjoyed.

I had brought the paper with me. I opened it to its title page. "The Problem of Li T'ang," I read. "By Matthew Karp."

I concentrated on Matthew Karp. I summoned up a thin, pale face. I added wild, untidy hair, a dirty T-shirt, crumpled jeans, and wire spectacles. I recalled an attitude of intense and, after the first class, nearly wordless attention. "Karp," I heard him saying, as we introduced ourselves to one another. "Matthew Karp. With a K." Which was practically the last thing he had said.

Was this the picture of a plagiarizer?

I had no idea. Doubtless plagiarizers, like everyone else in our dubious world, come in all shapes and sizes.

So much for that. It had not got me very far. The next move was to examine the evidence.

I examined it. Binding, inexpensive. Paper, ordinary. Typing, uneven, not to say sloppy. Contents, overwhelming.

It would have been easier, I saw appreciatively, if he had tried to mix in a few sentences of his own, explaining why Chinese painting was beautiful, or why he liked it. The contrast between the true and the borrowed Karp would have been inescapable. Look on this sentence, I would have been able to cry vengefully, and on this.

But he hadn't. He'd been more skillful. He had stolen every phrase in his twenty weighty and intricate pages, word for word. It was going to be difficult to prove that he had committed plagiarism at all. The only way to prove it conclusively was to find out where.

I went to bed and slept deeply and contentedly. The next morning I drove to the university, first to my office and then to the library, to eliminate the obvious possibilities. I looked at Sirén. I checked Sickman. I went through the admirable little book by Susan Bush.

Nothing in them corresponded to "The Problem of Li T'ang." I hadn't expected that anything would.

That afternoon, after an inadequate lunch in the

cafeteria, I returned to the library stacks, but no longer to their relatively habitable upper regions; I descended to their gloomy and slightly dank bowels, never visited by the light of the sun and rarely by the foot of man, in search of periodicals. I inspected bibliographies, located references, and pulled down dusty cardboard folders containing forgotten offprints. The one colleague I saw passed by as I was reaching for a journal tucked behind another journal on a top shelf. She produced a faintly worried smile and hurried on. That strange, sarcastic Dr. Harris was going to slip his disk again.

I found out a good deal that day about Li T'ang. What there was, at any rate, to find out. The first sixty years of his life were a blank. Then, at the beginning of the twelfth century, he emerged into the limelight. The occasion was a competition for admission to the emperor's Painting Academy. The assigned subject, I learned from a useful five-page summary by Ellen J. Laing, was "A wine shop by a bridge surrounded by bamboo." The other competitors obediently submitted paintings of wine shops by bridges surrounded by groves of bamboo. Li T'ang, with the sort of imaginative stroke so admired by painting academies then and now, confined himself to painting the flag of a wine shop, at the head of a bridge, outside a grove of bamboo.

As he was enjoying the fruits of this triumphant demonstration that less is more, however, the Painting Academy collapsed, along with the fabric of northern society in general. The resilient Li T'ang, now in his seventies, fled south. A second anecdote illustrated his new adversities. In the mountains a brigand stopped him, demanding his life or his possessions. These turned out to consist chiefly of scrolls and paintbrushes. But fortune, in twelfth-century China, still favored the arts. The brigand, if not a connoisseur, knew what he liked; overcoming his first disappointment, he enrolled himself as a class of one and followed his aged teacher south.

In the south Li T'ang's hardships were not finished. In a sardonic poem he described the large, gloomy landscapes he would have liked to paint and their probable effect on customers:

I already know that such scenes will not attract
the eyes of today's people.
Most buy cosmetics and paint peonies.

But the inward resources of this elderly wanderer were not finished, either. In his eighties, in troubled times, in a new city, among the cosmetic-buyers and the peony-painters, he resumed work, caught the eye of the new emperor, and was readmitted to the new Painting Academy, southern branch. There was his late masterpiece, to prove that he deserved his success—*Wind in the Pines Amid Myriad Ravines,* which I had looked at that day in a dozen different reproductions, a vast, dark, brooding, monumental mountain face. And there were the two other landscapes—light, casual, dreamy—which didn't seem to be in the same style at all. Which hadn't, according to Matthew Karp, been painted by the same painter.

And there was I, with no more notion of the source he'd plagiarized from than I'd had before.

Which was a relief. My instincts had told me from the start that this was going to be a subtle contest. And my instincts are always right.

The following morning was a class morning. My opponent and I were to meet face to face.

I drove to the art department, unaccountably housed in the chemistry building, and parked my yellow Porsche in the lot. I gave a warm greeting to the art department's thin, middle-aged secretary— there is a thin, middle-aged secretary at the heart of every organization, and it is well to be on her good side—and went upstairs to my classroom, temporarily cleared of Bunsen burners.

I did not give one of my better lectures. These required some preparation; my researches of the previous day had not left much time. I found myself relying more heavily than I would have liked on my own sources—Sirén, and when possible, Bush— and observing the third row for signs of guilt and confusion on the face behind the wire spectacles.

Perhaps it was a shade paler than usual. Perhaps the attention it was displaying was a shade more intense. Perhaps.

"Mr. Karp," I said, after the buzzer had sounded.

I had made it clear from the outset that I was not one of you new, matey, with-it teachers, anxious to be my pupils' chum. Our encounters were conducted with classical formality. We were "Mr." or, as the case might be, "Miss." Not even "Ms." Certainly not "Matthew."

It seemed to me that my antagonist jumped a little.

"Sir?"

I regarded him blandly. "Would you be so good as to come to my office for a conference at 10 o'clock tomorrow morning?"

It was perfectly proper for him to look nervous at the prospect of a conference. All of my students, at least all of those who had handed in their papers on time, would be conferring with me nervously during the next week or two. But I had picked him out first, a trifle pointedly, and for no evident reason.

It seemed to me he looked a bit too nervous. I was gratified to note, however, as he left the room, that I wasn't sure.

There was one move left. Plagiarism was not a topic to bring up lightly in academic circles. I could not go about asking casually if Matthew Karp was likely to have committed it; it was too grave a sin. But I could inquire of my fellow members of the art department, in the cafeteria, or the men's room, or in our other byways, if they happened to have had a Karp in any of their classes. Matthew Karp, with a K.

Several of them, after their surprise at being

approached by the unsociable Dr. Harris, admitted that they had.

What sort of a student had he been?

Their eyes brightened. Their voices lost their customary tones of complaint. Fine young man, they said. First-class scholar. Top-grade mind. Reminiscent glows lighted their faces as I turned brusquely away.

Had he been taking in every one of them?

Handing in a succession of fraudulent papers?

Masquerading his way through the art department?

Anything, I was aware, was possible. But as I stretched out that evening in what my real estate agent had called my conversation pit, it didn't seem probable.

Matthew Karp could hardly have bamboozled so many for so long. Yet he hadn't written that paper. I was almost certain he hadn't. All my instincts told me he hadn't, and my instincts are always right.

I opened it once more. Now that I had untangled most of its Germanic syntax, it was somewhat less difficult going. It even rang a distant bell. As if, somehow, I *did* know something about it.

As soon as I tried to work out where the bell was, its ringing vanished.

I began to feel uneasy.

At 9:55 the next morning I disposed what I like to think of as my lanky, Ivy League frame behind the desk in my office. From my tweed jacket, on the sleeves of which I had had a tailor sew leather elbow patches, I extracted a pipe, lighter, and pouch containing a black mixture specially prepared at a nearby tobacconist's. Through my window I looked out at the undergraduates perambulating to and fro through the bright October leaves.

How could I have imagined that academic life was dull? How could I have begun to wonder if it was time to move on?

I looked keenly at the closed door, by way of practice. I cleared my throat. "Come in," I said austerely, tuning up.

I glanced at the small traveling bag I kept packed in the corner, just in case.

There was a knock on the door.

I looked keenly at it. I cleared my throat. "Come in," I said austerely.

He came in.

There was no question about it. His face was paler. His hair looked wilder, his T-shirt dirtier, and his jeans more crumpled. He was in a state of controlled agitation.

"Sit down," I said.

He sat down on the only other chair, which I had positioned uncomfortably close to the corner of my desk. He attempted to find room for his legs, without success. He looked up, with a gaze that was not

only intense but squinting. Light flashed off his wire
spectacles.

"Sun in your eyes, Karp?" I inquired.

No "Mr." this morning. I sat forward, an inch or
two, in the insulting fashion of someone offering to
get up and pull down a window shade with no
intention of actually doing so.

"That's all right, sir," he said.

I sat back. The inch or two I had sat forward.
"Ah," I said irrelevantly. I allowed an empty silence
to grow, more and more pointlessly, in which he
was free to twitch, or bite his lip, or exhibit other
indications of cracking under the pressure of
increasing meaninglessness.

He did not move. Neither did his somewhat mag-
nified eyes. Instead, under his continuing regard, I
felt a desire of my own to change position, or cough,
or do something or other, no matter what. I checked
the impulse. But it was a warning.

"I asked you to see me, Karp," I said, "about your
paper." It was lying in front of me on my desk. I
pushed it away from me slightly with the tip of my
finger, the first suggestion that there might be something offensive about it.

He did not speak.

" 'The Problem of Li T'ang,' " I quoted. I paused.
"Tell me about the problem of Li T'ang."

He took a deep breath.

"I tried to, sir," he said, "in my paper."

I tested the ring of those words, silently, on

instant replay. Apprehension, yes. But not the panic I was listening for.

"Tell me again."

He took another deep, and slightly ragged, breath.

"Li T'ang was a landscapist. The most celebrated of all the Sung landscapists."

"What do we know about him?"

"He was born in the 1050s. He died in the 1130s."

That much was right, anyway.

"Go on."

"When he was in his sixties he was accepted into the Painting Academy. The assigned topic was 'A wine shop—' "

"Yes," I interrupted. "What else do we know?"

"After the fall of the northern Sung, when he was in his seventies, he went south. During his journey through the mountains he was held up by a—"

"Yes," I said. "What else?"

"He died in his eighties."

"And that's all we know about him?"

"We have a poem he wrote about—"

"A curious figure."

"Yes, sir."

"Elusive."

"Yes, sir."

"But one who landed on his feet."

"On his feet?"

"Wherever he jumped. In difficult times."

"I suppose so, sir."

I picked up my pipe. I put it down again.

"Tell me about his work."

"His style became the model for two generations of southern Sung painters. And that's the problem."

"What is?"

"What is his style?"

I regarded him.

"You tell me, Karp."

"On one hand, there's his great mountain landscape in the Palace Museum in Taiwan, *Whispering Pines in the Mountains.*"

My ears pricked up.

"*Wind in the Pines Amid Myriad Ravines?*"

"That's another translation, sir."

I relaxed. "Ah."

"On the other hand, there are two more landscapes attributed to him in a monastery in Kyoto. And they're completely different."

"In what ways?"

"They're airier. Freer. The brushstroke is different, the conception, everything."

All that was right, too.

"In that case," I said, "why not attribute them to someone else?"

"Because one of them seems to have his signature. The first character of his name may be visible, and the second character appears to show up in infrared photography."

" 'Appears to' ? " I repeated.

"Yes, sir."

" 'May be' ? "

"Yes, sir."

"Not exactly conclusive evidence."

"No, sir."

I shifted gears, to a slightly slower and more significant delivery.

"And a signature doesn't prove anything, does it?"

"No, sir."

"Anyone can take someone else's work and attach his name to it."

"Yes, sir."

"Can't he, Karp?"

He gazed at me, sitting rigidly in his chair.

"Yes, sir."

"Hm," I said. I toyed with a pencil. "What's your view?"

"I think that's what happened."

"What?"

"I think they were painted by someone else."

"Hm." I was beginning to repeat myself. I'd been waiting for him to give himself away with phrases from his paper, learned by rote. But he hadn't. He'd explained the question in his own words, so far as I could tell, and just as succinctly as I could have explained it. Perhaps more so. "Why?"

"I don't think they could be by the same painter as the landscape in Taiwan."

"They couldn't?"

"They're too different. I don't think they could be by the same *person*."

"Why not?"

"I don't think it's possible for a painter—for anyone—to turn into a different person."

"You don't?"

"No."

Ah, I thought, the certainties of youth.

"Even if he had to?"

"Had to?"

"To start again? In a new place?"

"If he could change that much—"

"Yes?"

"Like a chameleon—"

I thought I heard a quaver in his voice.

"Yes?"

"I'd feel sorry for him."

"You would?"

"Really sorry."

At last he was beginning to look upset. Somehow I had got through to him. I wondered how.

"Because he was able to adapt himself?"

"Because—"

"Yes?"

"Because he had so little self to adapt."

"But isn't that," I inquired, not wholly grammatically, "what an artist is?"

"What an artist is?"

"What all of us are?"

"All of us?"

"Chameleons?"

He clenched his hands.

"I don't think so, sir."

Somewhere I had touched a nerve. Where? But this was not the time for a discussion of identity crises in the modern world. It was time to come to grips with the situation, and the problem, *my* problem, was that I didn't know what to do next. I could not continue this interrogation much longer without its becoming apparent that that was exactly what it was, and at that point he would have every right, or *almost* every right, to get up, announce that he was not required to listen to any more of this, and walk out. Leaving matters twice as snarled as when he had walked in.

He unclenched his hands. I observed that he bit his fingernails.

I looked up.

"Why did you take this course, Karp?"

I meant the question to be unsettling. It wasn't. He had the fixed, desperate air of someone preparing himself for a last stand.

"I admired your book."

"You did?"

"Yes, sir."

I felt an inner tremor. If he admired that book, perhaps he *could* have written this paper. "You embarrass me," I said, waving a hand. "It was unreadable."

"Not at all."

"Ph.D. theses always are."

"Not that one."

"I looked at it myself, last summer, and could scarcely get through it."

"You couldn't, sir?"

"No."

"Really?"

"No."

"You're joking, sir."

"Certainly not. I never joke." I gave him a penetrating look. "And that's the reason you took this course?"

"That and my cousin, sir."

I stiffened slightly. Why was this new character being introduced into the drama?

"Your cousin?"

"Andrew Karp. He's in the art world, too."

I had been drawing something with the pencil on a sheet of paper. I saw that it was an airplane. A jet, in flight. I wondered what it meant.

I glanced up. "Have I met him?"

"I don't think so, sir." I looked down. That was a relief. "He's an assistant curator at the Met."

"He is?"

"He's a few years older than I am."

"About my age?"

"Yes, sir. But he doesn't look like you."

I glanced up again. Sharply. Why had he said that? "Why did you say that, Karp?"

"He looks more like me."

I continued to scrutinize him. Closely. There were hairs, I noticed, growing out of his nose. I decided not to probe the question any further. "Hm," I said.

"He's going to Taiwan this summer, and he's invited me to go with him."

"To the Palace Museum?"

"To arrange for the loan of three of their scrolls."

"I see."

"I wanted to be ready for the trip."

"I see."

"To know something about what I was going to look at."

I began a wiggly line underneath the jet. It looked like waves the jet was flying over. Perhaps my unconscious was trying to tell me something.

"So you'll have a chance to examine *Wind in the Pines Amid Myriad Ravines.*"

"Yes, sir."

"Or, if you prefer, *Whispering Pines in the Mountains.*"

"Yes, sir."

"An opportunity to settle the problem of Li T'ang."

"Yes, sir."

Our conversation seemed to be losing direction. I decided to get it at least partly back on the rails.

"You've never been there?" I asked carelessly.

"No, sir."

"But your cousin Andrew has," I added lightly.

"No, sir."

"They're acquainted with him, though."

"No, sir."

"They're not?"

"They've never met him."

Andrew Karp, about my age, the Met, Palace Museum, never met him. I filed it all away.

"I envy you." I had finished the waves the jet was flying over. I began a round-cheeked wind, blowing it westward. "I'd like to go there myself."

"You've never been to Taiwan either, sir?"

I thought rapidly. "Once. To do research."

"There must be nothing like seeing the real thing."

He sounded almost unhappy. Why?

"The real thing?"

"The paintings themselves."

"Oh."

"Instead of reproductions."

"I suppose so."

"Reproductions aren't the same, are they?"

"No."

"Even the best ones."

"No," I said. "I suppose not."

"May I ask you something, sir?"

I leaned back.

"That depends."

"When you were appointed to the art department, last summer, sir—"

I sat without moving.

"Yes?"

"Without being interviewed—"

"Yes?"

"Because of your slipped disk—"

"Yes?"

"Were you in a hospital, sir?"

"Yes."

"Would you mind telling me which one?"

I let a moment pass.

"Yes. I would mind."

He didn't speak. Neither did I. I let several moments pass, while we both sat without moving.

"Is that all?" I said.

"Yes, sir."

"Is there anything else you'd like to know?"

"No, sir."

"You're sure?"

"Yes, sir."

"Very well. There's something I'd like to know."

"Yes, sir?"

"About this paper."

"Sir?"

"This paper is magnificent. Almost impossible to read, of course. Because of its wretched writing. And arriving, in my judgment, at the wrong conclusion. But superbly researched, splendidly argued, and authoritatively presented."

I paused.

"Thank you, sir."

I leaned forward.

"Who wrote it?"

He leaned forward, too. That wasn't right.

"You did, sir."

That certainly wasn't right.

"I beg your pardon?"

"It's Chapter Seven of your book."

"Ah."

I stood up. I began to put pipe, lighter, and tobacco pouch into my pockets.

"I'm sorry, sir." He was still addressing me as "sir." Good. "I didn't think you were real from the beginning. With that pipe that you never smoke, and that tweed jacket with the elbow patches, and the whole old-fashioned, Ivy League bit." Ah, well. At least it hadn't been my lectures. "And your lectures. They were just paraphrases. Of Sirén and Bush." I stopped listening and started calculating. No time to go back to the apartment. Leave the Porsche in the parking lot. It wasn't paid for, anyway. The nearest form of public transportation was a Greyhound bus. And then—

Why not? A few letters, a passport, a discreetly trendy New York suit, and I'd be equipped.

He was still talking, more and more anxiously. "I couldn't ask you about it. I couldn't ask anyone about it. It was too—too awful." He halted. "But I had to find out. And this seemed like the only way." He seemed increasingly distressed. "I couldn't let you get away with it, could I, sir?"

"Of course not, Karp," I said soothingly.

"I think if I knew which hospital the real Dr.

Harris was at, and called them up, I'd find out that
he's still laid up somewhere with a slipped disk."

"Very likely." I looked around the office. "We
weren't able to do much for him."

"I think that's how you got this impossible idea of
coming here in his place."

"Yes." I picked up my traveling bag. "Goodbye,
Karp."

"I think you need help."

"Help?"

Was this an offer of assistance?

No. He was standing barring the door.

"I think you were a patient at that hospital."

"What?" I was stung. "A patient?" I couldn't let
that go by. "Certainly not. I was the head surgeon."

"You were?" His voice faltered slightly.

"Certainly." Perhaps a little more accuracy was
called for. "For three weeks." I reached past him for
the doorknob. "And I don't need help. You do."

"I do?"

"You're wrong about the problem of Li T'ang." I
turned the doorknob. "It's not only quite possible to
turn into a different person." I opened the door. "In
these uncertain times—" I stepped through. "It's
essential."

I closed the door behind me and walked briskly
down the empty corridor.

"Karp," I said to it, smiling cordially, striding forward, gripping my traveling bag, feeling the familiar
rush of blood to my head, on my way to the Palace

Museum in Taiwan, a few months ahead of time, to arrange for the loan of three of their scrolls. Perhaps more. Six. A dozen. "Andrew Karp. With a K."

Who has been, I may say, a very pleasant, amiable, undemanding person to be.

Until the day before yesterday, at the end of the second week of my visit, when the Palace Museum received word that another Andrew Karp, no doubt alerted by his cousin Matthew, is to arrive this afternoon to make sure that the eighteen scrolls to be loaned to the Met are delivered to the real Andrew Karp.

If there can be said to be such a thing as the "real" Andrew Karp.

Or "reality."

But that is hardly a topic I can touch upon when I disclose, to the rather excitable director of the Palace Museum, half an hour from now, my current, challenging, and possibly extremely brief assignment as an agent of the U.S. State Department sent from Washington to try to clear the problem up.

GERALD TOMLINSON

HIZZONER'S WATER
SUPPLY

Joe Skaggs hot-wired a Matador in a factory park-
ing-lot in Paterson and took it on a roundabout
back-street route to the rear of the Palladium Diner
in Kearny, just off the Jersey Turnpike where he
ditched it in front of a pair of green dumpsters. The
smell from the dumpsters could hardly spur business at the Palladium Diner, but Skaggs was not
there to eat. Pulling the collar of his windbreaker up
against the October chill, he leaned into the frigid
breeze and headed toward the area where the eighteen-wheelers were parked.

This stolen-car-to-truckstop routine was part of
Skaggs' modus operandi. He researched his heists
and followed the driver on his routes, observing his
habits, sometimes for as long as three or four weeks.

It was well worth it. The cargo in one of these trailers could pay for a lot of nights in Las Vegas—as long as he stuck to blackjack and avoided the slots. Of course, like any hijacker, Skaggs had to settle for a small fraction of the stolen goods' actual worth. *C'est la vie.*

He moved quickly along the asphalt, his shadow shifting in the glare of lights. The trucks were parked far away from the neon-bejeweled diner. The truck he was after, a Galen Lines rig, would be carrying a full load of electronic games and toys from a Baltimore factory to the stores of Boston just in time for the holiday season.

Skaggs knew nothing about electronic games and toys, but he did know how to drive a truck. After dropping out of Eastside High School, he had invested the modest haul from a gas-station holdup in a truckdriver-training course. The truckers' school, licensed though it was, taught him very little except the prevalence in the world of yet another scam. Even so, with the schooling behind him, he landed a job with a long-distance trucking outfit. The leathery old driver he was teamed up with soon taught him how to handle a rig.

The work made him nostalgic for holdups. It took him hardly any time at all to discover that long-distance trucking could rattle your teeth out in two years and disembowel you in five. Not only that, but buying the rig that would jar loose your teeth and innards cost upward of fifty thousand dollars.

No, thanks. There had to be a better way—and Skaggs found it. Hijacking trucks, not driving them. When a hijacking was well planned, carefully timed, and boldly carried out, it paid off handsomely. Skaggs had a long-time reliable fence, the fence had a warehouse in the wilds of Secaucus, and the warehouse had a loading dock awaiting the arrival of the games and toys.

It should go without a hitch. Technically it wasn't even a hijacking, just a truck theft. The driver, Bernie Carbone, was by now anchored to a stool at the Palladium's counter, working his way through liver and onions, battery-acid coffee, and gluey red pie. Skaggs had studied Carbone's route and schedule and knew them down to the minute. He had a good half hour to cover the three miles to Secaucus, unload the truck, and drive it to his ditching point near Teterboro.

A jumbo jet, the kind copywriters have dubbed wide-bodies, thundered above him, its myriad lights gleaming, its nose aimed at Newark Airport. A bitter wind lashed Joe's face. He ignored the din and the knife-edged cold as he slipped alongside the trailer in Carbone's usual parking spot. This was it all right, the big kelly-green rig, its engine idling.

Skaggs swung easily into the cabover tractor, snapped on the lights, released the brakes, slid the rig expertly into gear, and pulled away. Nothing could be easier, he thought. He wondered why half the eighteen-wheelers at the Palladium didn't meet the same fate. No, not really—he knew better than that. A lot of the Palladium customers were long-distance haulers with a second trucker asleep behind the cab.

The big Galen Lines truck roared east on the Pulaski Skyway, then north on Routes 1 and 9, its headlights piercing the crystalline night. At the Secaucus exit Skaggs pointed the rig down gloomy back roads, past blackened factories and hulking warehouses, until, at the one he wanted, he whipped the wheel sharply to the left. A massive door slid open in the building he had reached, and almost without slackening speed he disappeared into the waiting cavern. Down went the door.

He backed the trailer up to a long loading dock at one side of the building. On the platform stood half a dozen kids, eager and expectant, like something out of *Oliver Twist*, ready to set a Secaucus speed record for unloading a truck. To them it was late-night fun and fast bucks. Maybe it was even legitimate.

Beside them, looking tolerably like Fagin, stood Sid Gold, the reliable fence. Gold was a volatile little man pushing seventy, with a surprisingly stentorian voice for such a twerp. He had a cranium shaped like Mt. Kilimanjaro, complete with snow-capped peak. A strange elf was Mr. Gold, greedy but good-hearted in his way too, a manipulator par excellence, a man for whom the manipulation itself seemed to be the joy, the goal, the all-consuming passion. Not that he shied from driving a hard bargain. The bargains he drove were among the hardest, but they were also the safest.

A tough sprite if ever there was one, he had taken two big falls for fencing stolen goods while his suppliers, Skaggs and the others, never felt the heat. Gold seemed to pretend that the goods had fallen from heaven. He marveled at the existence of all that stolen stuff in his warehouse. He simply couldn't believe it, he told the judges. The judges had trouble believing it too.

Joe Skaggs jumped down from the cab and raced back to the dock. One of Gold's boys had begun to torch the lock and soon the doors swung open.

Gold stepped inside, nimble as a goat.

Ten seconds later he stepped out, back onto the dock, his wizened face drained of color, his deep voice issuing a command:

"Get this rig out of here."

Skaggs stared at him, startled.

"What?"

"Take a look."

Worried, Skaggs vaulted to the dock and examined his cargo. Electronic games and toys it was not. Every carton in the trailer, front to back, top to bottom, said BLISS in blue block letters on white cardboard. Below the trade name, in smaller type, appeared "Berkowitz Pharmaceuticals, Inc., Upper Darby, Pa."

"I don't get it," he said to Gold. "This is Carbone's truck."

"Get it out of here."

"Hey, Sid. Are you kidding? Bliss is worth—"

"Can it. Bliss is worth zero to me. Worse yet, it's a
prescription drug. A strong tranquilizer, somewhere
between Valium and Thorazine, I think. That's all I
need is a drug rap. Stolen toys, okay. Stolen drugs,
no way. Move the rig out."

"Listen, Sid—"

"Nothing doing, pal." As he said it, a big gorilla
named Bannon moved to his side and started glow-
ering. Gold, who had the strength of a toothpick,
needed an enforcer, and Bannon was his man. Bannon slammed and latched the truck doors. Gold
said, "Get that load of tranquilizers on the road.
Quick."

"I've got to fence it."

"You can't fence it, Skaggs. You got no contacts in
the drug trade. Don't be stupid. Ditch the truck and
get clear of it as fast as you can."

"Sid, it's worth a fortune, this load! I've got
enough Bliss here to tranquilize the East Coast for a
month!"

"It's your problem, pal."

Gold turned on his heel, motioning Bannon and
the kids to follow him. A moment later the huge
warehouse door yawned quietly open.

Skaggs, struggling to stay calm, rammed the
transmission into gear and roared out into the

smelly Secaucus night. He careened to the left, just as he would have done with an empty truck, heading toward Teterboro.

He had to think, but thoughts gridlocked in his brain. What should he do? Here he was hauling a fortune in the prescription drug Bliss. There had to be a market for it. But Sid Gold was right. Skaggs had never dealt in drugs, and he had no place to turn.

He made good time to Teterboro. Traffic was light, the traffic lights were on his side, and no patrol cars of any kind showed up ahead of him or behind him. He rolled onto a side road he had picked to abandon the empty rig.

And then he thought of it! Just as he was pulling to a stop in an ad-hoc truck-parking area, just as he saw the blue-and-white pay telephone, he recalled his angry remark to Gold: "I've got enough Bliss here to tranquilize the East Coast for a month!"

Yeah! Why not? Maybe not the whole East Coast, when you got right down to it. Maybe only one city—say, New York City.

Skaggs whistled. The pieces fell into place. He had practically been born to the job. Why hadn't he thought of it before? He'd been born and raised in Kingston, New York, a town a few miles east of the vast Ashokan Reservoir, one of more than twenty main sources of drinking water for New York City.

Forget selling the stuff. Skaggs' new game was blackmail. He would park the rig near the shore of

Ashokan Reservoir—hidden from view, of course—
he knew every foot of the desolate shoreline—and
then demand—how much? A million dollars? No,
he should take inflation into account. Make it three
million. Pay Joe Skaggs three million dollars, Mr.
Mayor of New York, and your citizens can go on
drinking water from the tap. Refuse to pay it and—
ha!

But he needed time. He needed it desperately.
Light traffic or not, it would take him a good two
hours and forty-five minutes to drive to Ashokan
Reservoir. Long before that, Bernie Carbone would
have wiped his chops at the Palladium Diner and
alerted the state police. The Galen Lines rig, even
with all the luck in the world, would never get
through to Newburgh, never mind Kingston.

But Skaggs still had an ace to play. He liked to
think he always had a spare ace. This ace's name
was Suzy, and she waited on tables at the Palladium
Diner. A few years ago Joe and Suzy had a thing
going, but then Joe got busted for hauling hot cigarettes, Suzy met a Purolator driver, and the affair
was off. But they stayed friends. Suzy knew about
Joe's heists, even though they rarely took place at
the Palladium. That this one had could save the
day.

He phoned the Palladium and asked for Suzy.
The manager had a strict rule about personal phone
calls, but it got violated about six times a night.

Over the clatter of dishes Skaggs heard her thin, sweet voice. "Hi." It sounded questioning.

"Suzy, baby. This is Joe—yeah, Joe Skaggs, not one of the other ten Joes you know. Hey, Suzy, I've got a job for you."

"Terrific. What does it pay? Can I give notice?"

"I mean it, baby. Is Bernie Carbone still there? . . . Yeah, I know he's good-looking. You been sweet-talking him a little? . . . Listen, could I ask you to do a little more than that? For pay?"

Suzy said, "Joe, I like you, but I draw the line at that. I got me a steady guy now."

"No, no, no, Suzy. Nothing like you're thinking. Just a mickey to give the poor guy some rest. He's working too hard. Maybe some of your Fiorinal would help. You're still using it, aren't you? Slip three or four of them in his coffee while you're gazing deep in his eyes and telling him he's the trucker of your dreams. Keep him in the diner, away from the parking lot. I need three hours, baby. And, hey, I'll never ask you to do it again. Just this once. It's worth a hundred bucks."

He heard her breathing into the mouthpiece for a while. "It's worth more than a hundred, Joe."

"Two."

"Three. A hundred dollars an hour. That's only fair."

Skaggs' knuckles whitened around the receiver. Yeah, but what can I do? he thought. "Okay, three. You got it. Just don't mess up. If he walks out of that greasebin before three A.M. yours truly is back in the coop."

"I'll do it, Joe. You know how I like you."

"Yeah."

He slammed down the receiver, remounted his cab, pored over the New Jersey and New York road maps from the glove compartment, and took off.

He had cause to worry. Suzy might or might not come through. If she blew it, he could expect to see the state police soon, probably before he reached the New York State line, certainly before he reached the reservoir. As the truck rumbled north on Route 17, he realized all too vividly where he should have been—back in Paterson counting money, phoning his travel agent to book him on a flight to Vegas. Instead he was jockeying a stolen eighteen-wheeler north, hoping, imploring that Suzy was earning her three hundred dollars.

The cab of Carbone's truck looked like the cockpit of a jet airplane. Anything electronic that was available to truckers, Bernie had it. Communication to and from the outside world was well provided for, but Skaggs would use a pay phone to call the mayor with his three-million ransom demand.

As the minutes passed and the miles rolled by, it began to look as if Suzy had done her job. Skaggs continued to bowl north on 17 and then, past Harriman, on 9W. He never received more than a bored glance from the few troopers he saw, never heard anything bothersome on the CB. He kept wheeling.

No interruptions. He was beyond Newburgh now. He could hardly contain his elation. He was going to make it. Less than fifteen miles more. They were fingernail-chewing miles, but they passed. Ten. Five. And there he was in Ashokan.

He peeled triumphantly off 9W onto Route 28, and then onto the well remembered back road of his childhood. You *can* go home again! he thought, finding the spot he had pictured in his mind, steering the rig off the road, across the packed earth, and trundling it down behind a dense stand of hemlocks. He backed and maneuvered the trailer into a small clearing, almost a natural garage, where it couldn't be seen from the road or the reservoir.

Time to get some rest, he told himself. There was no need to repeat the advice, no need to hasten it with Bliss. Within moments he was sound asleep, dreaming of the Vegas Strip, of aces and face cards, of chips and chippies.

He awoke with a start. The sun was up, glinting off the rippled surface of Ashokan Reservoir. Bluejays chattered outside the cab. When he opened the door a rabbit bounded away through the trees.

Today meant action, no time to waste. No matter how much Fiorinal Suzy had slipped to Bernie Carbone, the guy had come around by now and was shouting his loss to the world. It was time for Skaggs to follow up on that loss—which would probably get a little news coverage—with his own update, his own tough but reasonable request: Give me three million dollars, Mr. Mayor, and we can part friends. If you refuse, I'll turn the city into a simpering, spaced-out bunch of walking zombies.

There was a diner two miles back with a pay phone outside. He needed both. He walked the two miles, his windbreaker collar pulled up, passing half a dozen bare-legged joggers on the way. He hoped they stuck to the highway and didn't go wandering down among the sheltering hemlocks.

After a breakfast of bacon and eggs and toast, he put in a long-distance call to Sam ("My Door Is Always Open") Hoffman, mayor of New York. He got a flunky on the other end. He demanded the mayor and got an argument from the flunky.

Skaggs said, "Listen, Gofer, I'll tell you where we stand. I'm sitting at the edge of a New York reservoir. A big one. Now what I'm suggesting is this—a truckload of Bliss in the reservoir. Got it? You want to drink water down there in New York? Go ahead. Put on a happy face. Go bonkers on Bliss.

"Now, let me tell you, Gofer—and get it straight—there's a way around this. It's spelled m-o-n-e-y. It adds up to three million dollars. That's what I want. That's what it'll take to keep New York's Finest and everybody else in town from floating off to dreamland.

"I know you can't raise that kind of money yourself—you're on the mayor's coffee run and they hardly ever slip you a briefcase full of money—so let's leave it at this: you tell Sam Hoffman that I called. Tell him I'll call again in a couple of hours. Tell him to think of that three million bucks and to weigh it against seven million members of the Undead he's going to get otherwise. Okay? Good boy! Over and out."

He felt pleased about that talk even if he hadn't gotten the mayor's ear. He soon would get it. Meanwhile, he had time to kill. It was a four-mile round trip to the rig and he saw no reason to be traipsing back and forth between his fortune and the phone. He walked a short distance on a side road, sat down on a bale of hay, tried to ignore the autumn chill, and wished he had brought a pack of playing cards.

In two hours he tried phoning the mayor again. This time the flunky put him through to an aide.

"I want the mayor," Skaggs told the aide.

"You're speaking to Tom Feeney, you've probably heard of me. I'm an aide to the mayor. I can relay any message to him that's important."

"Well, listen, Tom. This message is important— I'm not trying to become a telephone pal of you folks. I've got a truckload of Bliss . . . yeah, the truck from Kearny . . . and I'm getting ready to flip the stuff in Hizzoner's water supply. It's going to cost him three million in used hundred-dollar bills to keep that water pure. To keep it from fuzzing up lads' and lasses' minds so that they all start thinking they're oh too wonderful for words—"

"Hold it a minute," Feeney snapped. "I don't

know whether you're a crank or a clown or a wig, but let me tell you this: the mayor has a few real problems to deal with this week. You may have heard. The garbage strike. The inmates' riot at Riker's Island. The bombing of a Russian diplomat's car on Second Avenue. The downgrading of the city's bonds. He doesn't need any bubbleheaded threats about Bliss in the city's water supply. I mean, I'll tell him you called. And I'll let the police commissioner in on our little secret. But my guess is you're not going to get a single greenback dollar."

Skaggs said slowly, "Tom, you're making one big bad error in judgment. I can turn a lot of minds to mush. When you chat with your boss, you tell him that. I'm through dealing with second and third bananas. Unless the mayor himself comes on radio and television tonight—"

"You're in luck, Mr.—"

"Keep talking."

"He's having a press conference at nine o'clock tonight to discuss the garbage strike and other matters. It'll be on TV and radio."

"Hey, fantastic, Tom. No need to be so formal about it, but it's his choice. You tell him to promise me the three million at that press conference, and I'll be in touch with him—or even you—to make the arrangements. All will be fine at the old water hole. If he *doesn't* promise the money, then, well, I'm sorry, but it's Bliss in the drink by midnight. You can count on it, I'm ready to unload. I'll be tuned in at nine."

"How do we know you've even got the Bliss?"

"I've got Bernie Carbone's rig, Tom. With the leopardskin seat covers and the diagonal crack in the lower left windshield. New Jersey license 397 XRV. Sound right? You bet."

"The police are looking for you right now, my friend. They'll find you before nine o'clock."

"You know better than that, Tom. There are reservoirs scattered all over the state. They'll never find me in time."

Feeney warned, "The mayor may not say anything about this on the air."

"He'd better. Otherwise it's going to be Happy Hour all over New York for a long, long spell. Understand?"

"I'll keep it in mind. I'll talk with the mayor this afternoon."

"I'll be tuned into the nine o'clock news conference. He agrees, or I fling pills."

"I heard you the first time. Something else—"

"Nothing else, Tom." Skaggs hung up. It would be dumb to be traced on the phone through long-windedness.

He started back toward the rig, confident the mayor would spring for three million dollars rather than risk watching the Big Apple turn into the Big Lullaby. He knew the mayor was a gutsy sort, up against it, up against his critics all the time. He knew that with his temper and temperament, he wouldn't take kindly to blackmail, but what choice did he have? Did he want liquid Bliss spouting from the tap? He'd have to agree to Skaggs' terms for the health and safety of the voters.

Back in the cab, Skaggs leaned back and waited patiently. He munched on sandwiches he'd bought from the diner. He listened to the multispeaker stereo AM/FM and some of the country-and-western tapes. He had no need to listen carefully until nine o'clock.

Late in the afternoon a couple of helicopters whirred low overhead, back and forth, back and forth, but they had no real hope, if that was their mission, of picking out the green rig under the green hemlocks.

As the hour approached, Skaggs found himself feeling a little nervous. What if Tom Feeney hadn't relayed the message? What if they didn't really believe he was the man with the Bliss? What then?

Nine o'clock.

The mayor spoke. He talked about the garbage strike. He went on and on. The negotiations were a mess, he said, just like the streets and just as smelly. He sounded haggard. He mentioned Riker's Island. The situation was worse than they thought—one guard had been killed, another mutilated. He sounded teary. He deplored the bombing of the Russian diplomat's car. It had been illegally parked,

undiplomatically ticketed, and blown to smither-
eens. There were casualties. He sounded contrite.
He tried to gloss over the downgrading of the city's
bonds, but a newsman hounded him. Yes, he admitted he had heard about it and he was disappointed.
He sounded angry.

Another newsman asked, "Wasn't there a phone
conversation this morning with the man who stole
the truckload of tranquilizers over in Jersey?"

The mayor took his time answering. "You know,"
he said thoughtfully, "things are falling apart in this
city. There is a quiet rage growing in many of us. We
would like to forget our fears, our concerns. But we
can't. So here, this morning, we have this very odd
character, no doubt from out of town, who wants to
blackmail us into clearheadedness. He wants to
charge us three million *not* to forget our cares and
worries. Is he crazy? Has he walked across Forty-
second Street? I say, let's smile again, New York.
Let's have a ball. To that poor misguided hijacker,
wherever he is, I say (*bleep*)."

Laughter.

"Does that mean no, Mayor?"

"That means no, fellows. No ransom money. So
there—go to work, you phantom pill-pusher in the
big green truck. Do your worst. Anything else?"

"About the threatened transit strike, Mayor—"

But Skaggs was not listening. He already had the
back of the truck open. His breath came like puffs
from a steam locomotive. His face was the color of a

turnip. He had said he would dump it all by midnight.

At six in the morning, with the first streaks of dawn lighting the sky, he was still opening cartons and pill bottles, his fingers torn and bleeding. His face had gone from purple to ashen, but his resolve burned on. At six-thirty he heaved the last fistful of Bliss into the water and dropped down beside the reservoir, beaten, bloodied, and exhausted. He fell asleep on the dewy grass. He had not taken a single pill himself.

New Yorkers went on about their lives as usual. They did not rush to buy bottled water. They did not flee the city for the tainted wells of New Jersey or Connecticut. They stayed, they laughed, they loved, they drank.

And Bliss reigned.

HENRY SLESAR

LIGHT FINGERS

There's one thing to be said for tyranny: it unites its victims. In the offices of the Stackpole Glove Company, intramural dissension was rare; the employees were firmly organized in their dislike of Ralph Stackpole, president and chief executive officer. Stackpole knew it, and Stackpole didn't care. Stackpole had learned something in 50 years of living and 30 years of the glove business, that the golden rule was: do unto others *before* they do unto you.

The morning that Stackpole discovered a thief in his organization began pleasantly enough. He had walked the six blocks from his apartment to the office, and the January frost had put an almost friendly glow on his seamed cheeks. He had been cordial to his wife at breakfast and polite to the secretary who brought him his mail. Even Blackburn, the office manager, whose nervous manner never failed to irritate him, got the benefit of a small smile when he entered the president's sanctum. The smile wasn't going to last.

"I can't understand it, Mr. Stackpole," Blackburn said. "Those model number 205's we ordered, the factory sent out a dozen samples, and all we have is eleven. . . ."

"Well, what can I do about it?"

"But it isn't just the 205's, Mr. Stackpole. Lately we've been having shortages that don't make any sense. It's almost like"— he paused the length of a nervous tic—"like somebody's been pilfering."

Stackpole gasped for air. "You mean I'm being robbed? Right in my own office?"

"Well, the way those gloves lie around the place, anybody could slip a box into a coat pocket or briefcase—"

The president stood up, his anger Jovian. "Nobody takes anything from me, Blackburn, understand? Nobody! I want you to find that crook and do it today!"

"Me?" Blackburn trembled. "But how? I wouldn't know where to begin!"

"Do you know how many pairs are missing?"

"Well, I'd estimate it at around six or seven."

"Yes, and for all we know it's a dozen. Or two dozen. And who knows what else he's been taking

around here? Stationery. Paper clips. My cigars!"
He flipped open the lid of his humidor. "Anybody
could walk in here and filch my cigars!"

"Of course, I could write a memo—"

Stackpole snarled with disgust. "Get out," he
said. "Don't send any memos. I'll handle this
myself."

Stackpole's method of dealing with the situation
was direct. He called in a private detective named
Semple and threw the problem at him. Semple, a
chunky little man accustomed to the troubles of
harried executives, listened attentively and asked:

"Just how serious is it, Mr. Stackpole? Doesn't
sound like you lost more than ten or fifteen dollars
worth of goods. Is that about the figure?"

"It's the principle," Stackpole said righteously.
"Nobody takes anything from me, Semple. Especially those people whose salaries I pay."

"Do you have any idea who it might be?"

"It could be anybody," Stackpole growled. "They
all look shifty-eyed to me. Maybe it's my own secretary. Or a mail clerk. Or maybe that good-for-noth-
ing Fred Cotter."

"Who?"

"Cotter. My designer. Young man. Bachelor, with
lots of girlfriends. Maybe they're all wearing my
gloves. I never did like Cotter."

"Then why do you keep him on?"

"Knows his stuff," Stackpole said ruefully. "He's
the best in the business when he works at it, but

half the time he's out of the office. Says he's going to 'studios,' but I know better. I wouldn't be surprised if he's the thief."

"Well, I wouldn't judge too quickly," Semple said sensibly. "Best thing to do in this situation is set a trap."

"A trap? What kind of trap?"

"I've used this method in some of the biggest firms in the country, and it's highly successful. You might say that it catches the culprit redhanded." He chuckled, and looked longingly at Stackpole's cigar.

"What do we have to do?"

"It's really very simple. Whenever you like, I'll bring in a supply of a fine, luminous powder with special clinging properties. We'll coat several glove boxes with the powder and place them strategically around the office, within reach of temptation. As soon as we've determined that some have been stolen, we conduct our inquiry with full confidence."

"Inquiry?"

"Yes. You see, the luminous powder will come off on the thief's hands, but he won't be able to see it except in the dark. Nor will it wash off his hands by any ordinary cleansing method. He'll be branded with his guilt as if he were tattooed."

"I get it," Stackpole snickered. "Then all I've got to do is take everybody into a darkened room and look for a pair of shiny hands." He leaned back in his swivel chair, his own eyes luminous. "It's a great idea, Semple. When can we start?"

"I could set it up this very evening if you like."

"One minute." Stackpole snatched the phone from its cradle and called his office manager. "Blackburn? We expecting anybody to be out of the office tomorrow?"

"No, sir."

"You sure now? Fred Cotter and everybody?"

"Yes, sir, everyone will be here far as I know."

"Fine," Stackpole said, hanging up. Then he grinned at the detective. "Have a cigar," he said.

That night, when the office was evacuated, Stackpole and his private investigator saw to the seeding of their plant. The president chortled gleefully as Semple coated the glove boxes with the white powder, and marveled at its near-invisibility. He insisted on extending the trap to his own cigar humidor, but that was as far as Semple would permit. At home, Stackpole described the arrangement to his wife; she had never seen him so exuberant before.

There was no business conducted out of Stackpole's private office the next day. He remained behind closed doors except for the lunch hour. Periodically, he checked with Blackburn to make sure that all personnel were about. Except for a secretary who was sent on an outside errand, a stock clerk who came down with an infected tooth, and a "studio" visit by Fred Cotter that lasted two hours, all were present and accounted for.

Until four that afternoon, Stackpole was filled with growing anxiety that the plot would fail, that the thief would elect to be honest that day. He was too impatient for a long siege: he wanted his victim now. And at four-fifteen, it appeared that he had him.

Blackburn telephoned.

"Mr. Stackpole?" His voice was hushed. "I just made a recount of the sample stack near the accounting department. There's a box missing."

"Are you sure?" Stackpole said, yanking the cigar out of his mouth. "You counted 'em carefully?"

"Several times. There were twenty-four boxes originally; now there are twenty-three."

Stackpole thumped his desk. "Everybody in the office?"

"Yes, sir. Mr. Cotter returned about half an hour ago, so everyone's here."

"Get 'em all into the large conference room at four-fifty, prompt. No excuses. I want hundred per cent attendance!"

"Yes, sir!"

Stackpole was uncontainable; no ingeniously profitable business scheme had ever excited him as much. By now he had forgotten Semple's role in the affair and thought of the scheme as his own.

When his employees marched into the window-less conference room at ten minutes of five, their faces were sullen. A mass meeting usually denoted a bawling-out, a limp holiday greeting at the end of the year, or a mournful report on profits. There were some titters from the girls in the secretarial pool, and a crooked grin on the face of Fred Cotter as he ambled into the room in shirtsleeves.

Stackpole went to the head of the conference table.

"Please let me have your attention," he said dryly, silencing the last shuffle and cough. "I've called you all together for the purpose of a little experiment. I want each of you to remain just where you are, and put out your hands so." He demonstrated, palms upward, fingers extended.

There was a buzz of curiosity, and some hesitation.

"Well, what are you waiting for?"

Every hand went out.

"Lights, Mr. Blackburn," Stackpole said.

Blackburn walked to the light switch, and flicked it. The room was darkened, and the surprised silence was broken by a ripple of nervous giggles.

"Mr. Stackpole!"

It was Blackburn's voice. Stackpole looked in its direction, and the sense of triumph that swelled in his chest almost popped his shirt buttons. For there, at the far end of the room, was a pair of brightly glowing hands.

"Lights! Lights!" Stackpole cried, pushing

through the crowd and clamping his fingers on the offender's arm.

Fred Cotter blinked at him. "What's the matter? What did I do?"

"So it *was* you!" Stackpole said ecstatically. "I knew I was right, I knew it! You thought you could get away with it—you thought you could cheat me—"

"What are you talking about?"

"Mr. Cotter, would you show me the contents of your briefcase?"

"Huh?"

"No, I don't suppose you'd be that stupid. You've probably gotten rid of the gloves already, haven't you? On one of your 'studio' visits." He whirled toward the office manager. "Blackburn, I want you to make up Mr. Cotter's check tonight. His discharge is effective immediately."

"You're firing me?" Cotter looked pleadingly at his fellow employees, but they were afraid to look back with sympathy. "I don't get it."

"You stole from me! You stole from the company! Do you deny it?"

Cotter flushed. "Okay, so I took a pair of gloves now and then. I didn't see any harm in it—"

"No, I don't suppose you did. Well, nobody takes anything from me, Mr. Cotter, it's too bad you didn't know that. You can clean up your desk tonight; I don't want to see you here in the morning."

Stackpole turned and glowered at the rest. Then his face softened.

"Goodnight, everyone," he said.

Stackpole spent the rest of the evening in his office, catching up on the work he had let slide during the day. It was too late for dinner at home, so he went to his club and enjoyed a solitary meal there. By the time he returned to his apartment, it was after eleven, and his wife was already preparing for bed.

"My, you worked late tonight," she said, slipping into her nightgown.

"How did your experiment go?"

"Perfectly." Stackpole chuckled. "And you know who the thief turned out to be? That no-good Fred Cotter!"

"Cotter? You mean your designer?"

"That's right; you met him at the Christmas party last month. The one who's always grinning. But I wiped the smile off his face tonight. I showed him that nobody takes anything from me!"

With a satisfied grunt, he crawled beneath the covers, and snapped out the bedside light. As he rolled over on his side he saw the luminous handprint on his wife's bare back.

TONITA S. GARDNER

IT'S ALL A MATTER OF LUCK

Ihe know I shouldn't have done it. And if I had to do it over again I'd think twice before I'd get myself into such a fix. Here's how it happened.

It was Sunday afternoon, and we were taking the kid to the airport to catch the flight back to State U. The kid's only seventeen, but her high-school record got her a scholarship. Besides a ninety-two average, she was captain of the girls' hockey team, president of the Stained Glass and Pottery Club, and co-chairperson of the April Fool Follies.

So we're driving along, the wife and I quiet because we're starting to miss the kid, who can't wait to leave. But as we pull into the airport, I'm so busy wondering how I can lose twenty pounds that I'm not tuned to what's going on until the kid pipes up. "Say, Dad, why aren't any planes taking off or landing?"

"Yes," says the wife. "It's awfully still for a big municipal airport."

They're right. I look out the window and what I see is even more spooky than no noise. Everywhere, people are standing around—business types with briefcases, old ladies holding shopping bags, sun-burned couples with tennis rackets in one hand and golf clubs in the other—all standing on the grass outside the terminals.

Something's peculiar, I tell myself as I edge the Chevy toward the departure area. I'm about to swing onto the upper ramp when a guy with a whistle comes scooting out from between the cars up front.

I roll down the window and ask, "What's going on?"

"Keep moving, buddy."

"Maybe it's a bomb," says the kid.

"Yes," the wife says. "There are so many nuts in this world."

"And look!" says the kid. "The buildings are empty!"

I poke my head from the car. "Excuse me," I call to a man near the roadway. "Is it a bomb scare?"

"You better believe it," he calls back. Before he can say more, a policeman with white gloves orders me to step on the gas.

I do, up till the exit, where there's a helluva jam.

Horns honking, brakes screeching, dozens of machines trying to wedge into the same space at the same time. But with all service roads barricaded by police, inbound cars can't enter. Slowing down, they block the way for those trying to leave. Meanwhile, as tempers boil over like unwatched spaghetti, drivers shout cracks about other drivers and their mothers and are told by even bigger loudmouths to do things no man can possibly do.

The wife solves the problem by closing the window. Tight. Mustn't contaminate the kid's ears. But the kid's got other things on her mind.

"Dad," she says, "how am I going to get back to school? Tomorrow's flights are booked and the bus won't get me there for my twelve o'clock class."

"First thing in the morning I'll drive you myself," I tell her, dreading the prospect of ten hours behind the wheel. "Now let's go home and relax."

We finally zigzag out of the traffic and we get home all right. But we don't relax. The side-door window's broken. Somebody was—or is—in the house.

I inch the door open.

"Don't go in," says the wife, holding on to the kid.

"They've gone."

"How do you know?"

I point to some stuff left behind on the doormat: the empty box from my gold-filled cuff links and a canceled bankbook closing out a $37.00 account.

"They could be hiding," she warns.

I step into the kitchen and, for her sake, poke through the broom closet.

"They may have guns!"

"Take my word for it—no one's in the house." I start for the stairs.

"Don't!" she shrieks. "They'll kill you, Ernie!" Pushing ahead of me, she runs upstairs.

I hurry after her. She speeds through the bedrooms and collapses on the bench in the hall. "There's no one here," she says, panting with relief.

"Why did you go ahead?"

She glares at me. "It's a free country. If anybody was here, I had as much right to be killed as you!"

I reach for her hand. With the kid following, we check all the rooms to see what's missing.

There's plenty—the color TV that I'm still paying off on time, the wife's service-for-twelve silverplate that was a wedding gift from her parents, and the kid's stereo that we wouldn't let her take to college because someone might steal it. Plus, as we check some more, a bunch of other things, from my first bowling trophy to my last bottle of Four Roses.

The kid looks stunned and the wife is shaking her head. "Can you believe it? They even took my eggplant casserole and a bag of Bartlett pears from the refrigerator."

I call the police.

• • •

"O.K.," I tell the wife as I hang up. "They'll be here soon."

"Are they going to look through the house?"

"Of course."

"Oh, my goodness!"

"What's the matter?"

"I didn't wash the bathroom floor this morning. And there may be a ring around the tub."

She goes to make the bathroom shipshape for the police while the kid grabs the phone to call her friends. "You should see what happened, Sue!"—"It's un*real*, Debbie."—"I mean, I can't describe it, Pam!"—

While I wait for the patrol car I remind myself that there are twenty-two houses on our block, all exactly alike. But the guy next door has a new Mercury in the driveway. Across the street they've got expensive awnings and a brick barbecue. The first one's a plumber, the second owns a fried-chicken franchise. Both earn a lot more than my three-chair barbershop. So why did the crooks pick *my* house?

I ask the detective after he dusts for fingerprints and can't find any except ours. He shrugs. "I guess it's a matter of luck."

When the cops leave I get an idea. "Listen," I say to the wife and kid, "we got our health, we got each other, and insurance covers part of the loss. So what are we stewing about? Let's grab a bite and take in that new Burt Reynolds movie."

"But there's a special on Channel Four," says the wife.

I remind her, as gently as I can, that the TV is gone.

We drive to McDonald's for burgers and shakes, and make it to the Cinema just in time. But they've changed the picture and raised the price. The theater is jammed and the couple in front of us are chomping popcorn like their upper teeth are mad at their lower. Then, when they finish eating and start pawing each other, the guy in back of us falls asleep. And—believe me!—he snores.

It's such a lousy flick, I don't blame him.

So I sit and watch the screen and realize that for the second time in one night we've been ripped of. But I still keep my cool.

When we get outside, cold rain is beating down. Thanks to the example I've set, nobody complains. We just shiver in silence and look forward to getting in the car and turning on the heater.

In the parking lot we find a front tire slashed.

"Consider yourself lucky," says a woman in the next car.

"Yes," says her friend. "They got *two* of ours. We're waiting for the AAA."

I don't consider myself lucky—and I don't belong to the AAA.

While the wife and kid huddle in the front seat, I

jack up the car. Rain pours down my collar and up my sleeves. Changing the tire, I step into a muddy pothole.

And that does it. With my feet as squishy as raw clams, I start cursing under my breath.

The wife and kid are tuned to my mood. As I get into the car, they don't say a word. I start the motor and head for home. We go a couple of blocks. I stop for a red light. Which doesn't turn green. So we wait.

Meanwhile, it stops raining. But the light is still red. I start easing the car out past the white line. There's no traffic along the side street, but I can't bring myself to go farther. Until the kid, who didn't get a ninety-two average for nothing, comes to the rescue. "Dad"— she points to a signal button on a nearby traffic pole—"look!"

She jumps out of the car, presses the button, and jumps back in. The light turns yellow. As it does, I plow across the intersection. And look in my mirror and see a police car zooming after me.

The man in blue waves me over and cuts in ahead. As he struts to the car, he wets his index finger and starts pawing through his ticket book.

"What're you tryin' to prove, fella? There are laws against goin' through yellow lights."

"Yes, sir." I don't dare deny it. "But we got caught in the rain and I wanted to get the wife and kid home before they catch—"

"Lemme see your license and registration."

I hand them over.

"Dad," says the kid, "he's writing out a ticket!"

"Oh, dear," says the wife. "This has been *some* day."

The lawman couldn't care less. Finished, he marches back to his car and speeds away. I blink at the souvenir he's left behind. Suddenly I'm so bushed that I just want to take off my soggy shoes, plop in front of the TV, and have a little nightcap. But the TV is gone, my booze is gone, and, for all I know, even the slippers I got for Christmas are gone. And there's still that ten-hour drive tomorrow—without a spare tire.

I reach out to turn on the ignition. Nothing happens.

I try it again. Still dead. The battery? It can't be. The battery is new.

I close my eyes, lean my head back, and tell myself it's a bad dream. Plus—my stomach is acting up—a bad case of indigestion.

"You're so quiet, hon," says the wife.

"Are we stuck?" asks the kid. She's ready to cry.

I haul myself out to check the wires under the hood. They're O.K. Again I try to start the car and can't. Meanwhile, making believe nothing's wrong, the wife decides to redo her lipstick. As she flips on the overhead light, I come face-to-face with the gas gauge. I stare at it.

The tank is empty.

"What are we waiting for?" says the wife.

"Come on, Dad," says the kid, "let's *go*."

And that's when I finally open my big mouth and say a lot of things I shouldn't.

As I walk the mile to the nearest gas station I'm still spouting words I hardly ever use, even when I miss a strike in a bowling tournament.

Not that it does any good. At the station, the kid attendant sizes me up. "Sir, I can't pump gas unless you've got the right amount of money." He explains how his father's afraid of robberies, so at night all cash goes into a locked strongbox buried under the floor.

A can rents for two dollars and the gas costs three. All I have is a ten-dollar bill.

"Maybe somebody can break it for you, sir." He points to a string of lights in the distance.

I head across the road to a small brick building lit by pink neon—ANGIE'S CHOP HOUSE. The door is locked and the place looks closed for the night. With my luck, it's what I expected. Then I notice a new Caddy parked to one side.

I bang on the door. I hear footsteps.

"Who's there?"

"A guy who needs change," I say. "For a ten, to be exact."

"Who is it?"

"I told you, Mister. I need change."

Louder. "What's your name?"

I don't know his. Why should I give him mine?

I'm about to say so when my galloping stomach reminds me of my dinner. "Big Mac," I say.

The door opens. A man in a black suit looks me over. "You're new, huh?" He fingers a wiggly scar on the side of his nose. "What happened to Weirdo?"

"Weirdo?" I shake my head. "I think you got me mixed up with someone else."

"O.K., I get the message. But why'n't you gimme your name right away?" Frowning at me, he scratches his scar. "Big Mac, huh?"

I pat my beefy middle. "That's me."

"Did the boss send you?"

I picture the boy in the gas station. "No, his son."

"Yeah—Junior's always rigging up surprises," says Scarnose. "Wait here." He disappears and comes back with a brown paper bag from the A&P. "Make sure to get home safe—if you know what I mean."

"What about my ten?" I remind him.

"You're getting what you're supposed to."

"I am?"

"It's in the bag, Mac." He hands it to me. "See ya," he says, and shuts the door in my face.

I look in the bag. There's nothing but a stuffed teddy bear.

Now I'm sure he's got me mixed up with someone else. I'm ready to knock again and give the man back his present when he opens the door again. His jacket is open too. And—talk about scared!—a gun is bulging from the inside pocket.

"The finks'll be on your tail, Mac. So you better beat it outta here. Fast."

I do. Fast.

At the gas station I gladly fork over my last ten dollars, figuring it's worth five extra bucks to be alive. Still holding the brown bag, I lug the can of lead-free to the car. By the time I get there, I've decided Weirdo's pal was putting me on and his gun was a toy. I feel like a jerk—and don't say a word about it to the wife and kid.

I drop the bag on the front seat and gas up the Chevy. As I get behind the wheel I see the kid has opened the bag and is taking out the teddy bear. "For me?"

"If you want it."

"Ooh, Daddy, he's a*dor*able." She hugs it. "Thanks a million!"

When we get home, she packs the teddy bear in her suitcase. I set the alarm and we all fall into bed.

At 3:00 A.M. I wake up in a cold sweat. Suppose Scarnose *wasn't* putting me on? I remember the airport and my stomach does a flip-flop. Maybe that bear is a bomb!

I hurry downstairs, zip it from the suitcase, and— no time for robe and slippers—rush outside with it.

Tearing down the street, I head for the drainage sump a couple of blocks away. But the moon is hiding behind a cloud, and if I stumble in the dark I could wind up as chopped meat. So I slow to a trot.

A neighbor's dog, usually busy dumping garbage cans at this hour, thinks I'm playing with him. With one giant bite he grabs hold of my pajama leg with his sharp front teeth.

"Scram!" I tell him. He rips off a big piece. I scoot away without it.

Tarzan is right behind me—catching up with the other leg.

"Let go, you stupid mutt!" I pull at him. "You'll kill us both!"

He lets go and starts to bark like I'm killing him.

Lights blink on in two or three houses. A window opens.

"Hey, stop that racket!" yells a neighbor. "And get your dog off the street!"

"It's *your* dog!" I shout back. I want to toss the bomb onto his lawn. Instead I keep going. So does Tarzan. While he nips at my knees, the pavement gashes my feet.

At the corner, I cut across a lawn to ease the pain. By now Tarzan's shredded my other pajama leg and I'm busy trying to hold the teddy bear and keep my pants up, so I don't see a hose curled in the middle of the lawn. I trip over it and land on my stomach— the teddy under me, the wind knocked out of me.

And—I breathe again—there's no bomb!

Tarzan slurps my face to show we're still friends,

sniffs at some azaleas, and goes to look for some garbage cans.

As I pick myself up, I see that the teddy bear has split open and some stuffing is hanging out.

I examine it under the streetlight.

It's green. And it's paper.

Sprinting back to the house, I reach into the teddy and dig out the rest.

I count it, tell myself it's a mistake, and count it again.

Ten thousand dollars!

Wondering what to do next, I figure there's no reason the kid can't keep the bear. I fill it with kleenex, decide she can sew up the seam when she gets to school, and replace it in her suitcase.

But I don't know where to put the cash.

And that's when it hits me. Without meaning to, I've stolen a lot of money.

As I said before, if I had it to do again I'd think twice before I'd get myself into such a fix. If I go to the police I could wind up in jail, and if I go to Scarnose I could wind up in cement.

So there's only one way to save my skin.

Until I can lose twenty pounds and grow a beard, I'll have to get out of town. Of course the wife'll come along, and as soon as school is out we'll send for the kid. With all the bad luck we've had, a ten-grand trip to Europe'll do us a lot of good.

THELMA C. SOKOLOFF

PROVIDENCE WILL PROVIDE

Everybody at Morgantown High School knew about Jessie Widmark's retirement plans. One of these days she was going to pack up her art books and her paint brushes, take her tiny pension, and live out her days comfortably in Cuernavaca. At least, that's what Jessie and the other faculty members thought until word came down from the mayor's office about the budget cutback of all teachers without tenure.

At first it didn't seem so bad. It was the young ones who'd be fired, and everybody said they'd probably get better jobs anyway. But then suddenly someone remembered Jessie—six months away from retirement and never tenured. Now there'd be no pension.

The principal, Dr. Stevens, called her in and broke the news. "I feel as bad as you do, Jessie, but there's nothing I can do. You know we couldn't give you tenure because you only went to teacher's training school. I always hoped you'd go back to college and get your degree."

"I surely meant to," Jessie said, "but there was always Mother to take care of, and the years just slipped away from me. Then, too, it was perfectly acceptable way back when I started teaching." Jessie stifled a small cough that was all that stood between her and tears. "Anyway, I didn't need tenure to get my pension—just had to work out my thirty years." Her voice trailed off. "Whoever thought I could be fired just months before retirement?"

"I've appealed to Mayor Billings, Jessie, but the mayor says he just can't make any exception."

"Jack Billings has a mighty short memory." Jessie's steady glance caught Dr. Stevens unaware. "I guess Jack's forgotten the year I passed him in everything even though his grades were failing. I knew his father was dying and I felt sorry for the boy."

Dr. Stevens rearranged the objects on his already neatly arranged desk. "Jessie, you're caught in a box of bureaucracy that's all tied up with red tape. It's not much consolation, but we'll be having a big retirement party for you. That's the least we can do."

Jessie Widmark's dismissal hung like a pall over

Morgantown High School. In a school filled with dull books and dreary staff members, Jessie's slightly offbeat personality was a joy. Everybody loved the small trim figure that scurried through the halls dressed from head to toe in one bright color. The sight of Jessie arriving on her motorscooter in the mornings was a high spot of the day, and an invitation to Jessie's apartment for a home-cooked meal of Tibetan delicacies was highly sought after.

One of Jessie's many contributions to the school was her little mottoes or "Jessieisms," as they came to be called. She had survived what she thought of as a healthy and productive life and felt it was her duty as a teacher to pass along bits of learning that she hoped would be helpful. Every day Jessie would write a little rhyme on the blackboard: *Start each day the hot-breakfast way; Stay close to a friend, don't borrow or lend;* or *Save a penny, soon you'll have many.*

As the years passed and Jessie began to look on herself as the elder stateswoman of Morgantown High School, she branched out with her little mottoes. Frequently she'd post a notice in the lunchroom to advise: *After you eat, keep our lunchroom neat* or *Protein in your diet? You really ought to try it.*

The students would giggle as each new Jessieism appeared and when they'd tell their parents, there'd be knowing smiles from the older generation who remembered the monochromatic outfits and the

motorscooter as well as the slogans when they were
in her class.

Jessie worked out her last weeks on the job,
presenting a brave but worried face to students and
faculty. "But with no pension, what'll happen to
your retirement plans?" Dorothy Abbott of Sociol-
ogy asked one day at lunch. *"There'll be a change in
the tide, and Providence will provide,"* Jessie
answered with one of her own mottoes. "Providence will provide."

The faculty and staff of Morgantown High went
all out in giving Jessie the banquet they'd promised.
Irene LaFitte's catering service was called in and the
gymnasium was done up in pink and green crepe
paper, with baskets of pink glads banked around
the dais. Everybody made speeches and Jessie was
presented with a gold watch and a lifetime subscription to the *National Geographic.* Of course, as Dorothy Abbott pointed out, at Jessie's age a lifetime
subscription wasn't going to bankrupt the Board of
Education.

The thing about the affair that made Jessie most
happy was the return of so many old students—
some of them she hadn't seen in years. There was
Melanie Potts, pushing 30 and still painting those
dreary still lifes. There was Jimmy Coughlin who'd
given up dreams of being a painter to take over his
father's cannery. And there was Danny Dumont,
always her favorite. Poor Danny, his golden fingers
had ended up repairing TV sets instead of creating

the beautiful sculptures Jessie had expected from him.

It was Danny who helped Jessie home with her gifts and packages and all the way he was silent. Finally, as they stacked the last box on Jessie's kitchen table he spoke. "You know, Miss Widmark, I've always remembered what you taught us—*Be honest and aboveboard, and you'll reap the reward.* Only problem is it's just not working for me. I'm the most honest guy around and my TV business is going nowhere."

"I'm sorry things aren't working out for you, Danny. Truly sorry. We'll have to get together and have a long chat soon."

After Danny left and she'd put her gifts away, Jessie poured herself a cup of tea.

She was already beginning to feel the loneliness she feared. It wasn't going to be easy, and Jessie knew it.

For the next few weeks she busied herself with errands and projects, but as the cold winter drew on and she sat alone in the small apartment, a bitter resentment began to creep into her chilled bones. The bright sun was drenching Cuernavaca with its warmth this very day; the bougainvillea was casting lovely shadows around the tiny cottage Jessie had chosen for her retirement. She had been treated shabbily and she knew it.

As Jessie thumbed through the evening paper, an item caught her eye. "Crime Wave Hits Morgan-

town; Mayor Billings Cautions Citizens." From the
back of her mind a bit of buried trivia bubbled to the
surface of Jessie's thoughts. Perhaps she could help
the mayor with his problem—help him in his job as
he had helped her. When she walked into the
kitchen to prepare another lonely meal, she looked
up Danny Dumont's number in the phone book.
She'd have to call him in the morning to come over
for that chat.

It was two days later when Jessie Widmark pulled
her purple cloth coat up around her neck, straight-
ened her small purple flowerpot hat, and knocked
on the door of Mayor Jack Billings' office. "Why,
Miss Jessie," Jack faltered. "I've been meaning to
come around and talk to you. Mighty sorry about
what happened with your job—dirty shame it was.
I sure wish I could have done something to help,
but we just had to lay off as many—"

"It's over and done now, Jack," Jessie interrupted,
"over and done. I came here about that item I read
in the paper. All those burglaries and things—looks
mighty bad for you as mayor, Jack."

"Well, I'm not happy about it, Miss Jessie. What
do you have in mind? You're not planning on playing Nancy Drew at your age, I hope." Jack Billings
cast a condescending little smile at Jessie.

She spoke slowly and thoughtfully. "I need
something to keep me busy, Jack. As you know, I
didn't *plan* to retire just yet, but that's another story.
I've been thinking how everybody in town knows

about my little mottoes and everybody knows I'm an artist—perhaps I can combine my talents, keep myself busy, and be helpful to the town too."

"I'm sure glad to see you're not bitter about losing your job. What do you have in mind, Jessie?"

"I'd like to make up a series of little signs to help with this crime campaign. You know—*A lock on your door makes burglaries a chore.* That sort of thing. I'd paint them myself and place them around town. There'd be no charge for my work and you'd be keeping an old lady out of mischief."

"Sounds like the town has nothing to lose," Mayor Billings said. "Go to it, Miss Jessie."

In the next few months Jessie Widmark's familiar figure was seen frequently darting about town placing the signs in strategic places. On the park lawn were the words: *Walk with a friend, and muggings will end.* In front of City Hall residents were advised: *Help a child stay alive, slow down when you drive.* On every bus in town Jessie posted warnings: *Give your wallet a thought, and help a pickpocket get caught.*

Several small notices appeared in the *Daily Bugle* informing readers of Jessie Widmark's ambitious little project. Eventually an editorial commended her on the unique service she was rendering. Unfortunately, however, the notice pointed out, the outbreak of small crimes persisted. If anything, the wave seemed to be reaching epidemic proportions.

And then as summer came to an end, a moving

van was seen taking away Jessie's few possessions, all packed up for shipping. The next day she headed for the airport where she noted the headline on the newspaper stand: "Mayor Billings Resigns in Furor Over Crime Wave." Jessie Widmark smiled as she boarded the plane for Cuernavaca.

The sun around the bougainvillea-shaded cottage was as warm as Jessie imagined it would be. A few miles down the road in a stucco-walled studio, Danny Dumont was working on a sculpture that Jessie thought had great potential. Frequently, when he'd drop by in the evening for a cold glass of tea and a dinner of Tibetan delights, Danny and Jessie would talk happily about their triumph.

"It was your little signs that really did it, Miss Widmark. What a stroke of genius that you remembered about people checking to see if their wallets were safe whenever they heard or read about pickpockets."

"Yes, Danny, but you had the golden fingers. You knew just how to lift the wallets without anybody being the wiser. I always knew you were wasting your time working on those TV sets."

"Why, it was a cinch." Danny smiled shyly. "Even for an inexperienced dip like me. Every time they'd look at your pickpocket sign on a crosstown bus, their hands would fly up to just where the wallet was resting. I never had to fumble—just go directly to the target. It's like you used to tell our class: *Life can be sunny if you don't lack for money.*"

"That's right, Danny." Jessie looked happily around the pleasant room. "And let's not forget: *All worries are past for the one who laughs last.*"

FRANK SISK

DOGBANE

I am not a loquacious dog. I do not bay at the moon nor bark at my own shadow. I do not pursue vehicles in motion, yapping witlessly and gnashing my teeth at tires. I am, as dogs go, a fair cut above the average. My young friend Jeffrey, if called upon, will attest to this.

Some of the AKC snobs look down their muzzles at me because I cannot accurately place my forebears. My dam, as I recall, was a fetching mixture of Airedale and Dalmatian, and she seems to have hinted at least once that my sire was a well-to-do Irish water spaniel. But who knows what goes with these bitches?

I was hardly weaned when, one fine day, I left

home for a bit of a prowl and then could not find my way back again. Ever since, I've been my own dog.

At first I found the going tough. Many a night I bedded down in an alley with an empty belly, but as I grew older and larger and wiser, I learned to provide for myself: another dog's bone here, a cat's dish of milk there, often a can of quality garbage, occasionally stuff strictly for the birds. And shelter? Well, all sorts of places—an abandoned car, a disused shed, an overturned crate.

Oh, I've wandered. Let's admit it, I'm a tramp.

Nowadays, though, I've more or less settled in the suburbs. I like it here for two reasons: dogbane is available and so is my young friend Jeffrey.

Let me tell you about Jeffrey first. He is a two-legger about my age, which is five summers, but like all two-leggers he is a mighty long time growing up. He is not yet half the size of his sire and dam. On his head he has a yellowish fur, but nowhere else; in his jaws he has very small teeth. His hands on my back are the gentlest I've ever known.

Jeffrey does not like certain foods, such as beef liver and oyster stew. As a result, I frequently enjoy these delicacies surreptitiously when the servant named Maude is not looking. It is this sort of deal that actually brought Jeffrey and me together in the first place.

I do not belong to him, of course. As I've already said, I'm my own dog—but I began hanging around here a few months ago. I sleep in what the two-leggers call a gazebo. Nobody bothers me. I come and go as I please.

Jeffrey calls me Big Dog. His sire calls me Mutt—he seems to regard me as a good-natured joke. I've never had an official name, like many of my species, but sometimes I have thought of myself as Ambrose. Don't ask me why.

Well, anyway, here I am with Jeffrey's companionship, interesting delicacies smuggled from his plate, and the shady comfort of the gazebo. Also, down at the far edge of the garden is a cluster of pink-flowering shrubs which Jeffrey's dam calls wild ipecac and honeybloom, but plain and simple dogbane is what it is. Whenever I feel depressed I chew a few of its pods and am almost immediately enveloped in a sense of euphoria. I become more perceptive. I am much better able to understand the complexities of the two-legger's jargon. In short, dogbane fixes me up much as a spot of alcohol uplifts the spirit of Jeffrey's sire.

So it is obvious I am now better off than ever before. I was basking in this thought just the other morning when Jeffrey emerged from the back door. He called to me and I came trotting. He took me around the corner of the house, where Maude could not see us, and took three breakfast sausages from his pants pocket. They were delicious.

After that we did what we often do—took a walk along the quiet street past the other large houses set far back behind white wrought-iron fences or solid walls of clay-colored brick. We walked as far as the corner, perhaps two thousand paces away, and then turned around to go back in accordance with the constantly repeated instructions of Jeffrey's dam: *Never cross the road.*

Just then an old station wagon pulled up to the curb and came to a stop beside us. A two-legger leaned across the front seat and spoke through the rolled-down window: "Hello, kid. Remember me?"

"Yes," Jeffrey said.

"Who am I?"

"You're Carl," Jeffrey said. "You used to drive Daddy's Rolls."

I recognized Carl, too. When I first arrived at the gazebo, Carl had been the family chauffeur, driving the big car only. A few weeks later, he dropped out of sight and a small brown two-legger took his place.

"Right you are, champ," Carl was saying. "Hop in and I'll give you a lift home."

"I'm walking with Big Dog," Jeffrey said.

"Forget Big Dog," Carl said in a tone I didn't like. "Hop aboard and I'll buy you some candy."

"I'm not supposed to do that," Jeffrey said.

"The hell you say," Carl said, opening the door suddenly and grabbing Jeffrey by the arm.

I leaped forward with a show of my teeth, which aren't bad for my age, and received from Carl a painful boot in the ribs. Before I could recover, the station-wagon door was slammed shut and then the evil-smelling thing roared away with my young companion. I chased it. By all that's canicular, I chased it—but I don't have the stamina of old, and shortly the thing vanished beyond reach of my eyes and nose.

As soon as I regained my wind, I rambled back to the gazebo and took a nap. I was wakened by Maude's voice calling for Jeffrey. Trotting down to the dogbane spread, I helped myself to a few pods. Right away I began to feel stronger and smarter.

Then Jeffrey's dam joined Maude in calling his name. At noon the sire entered the driveway in a squat little car and, with his mate, started a thorough search of the grounds.

Following at their heels, I barked Carl's name six or seven times.

"I think old Mutt is trying to tell us something," the sire said. "I've never heard him bark like this before."

"Carl's the culprit," I barked.

"Too bad he can't speak," the dam said.

"I am speaking," I yipped.

"I better notify the police," the sire said.

"Yes," the dam said, and they went into the house.

That's the difference between two-leggers and four-leggers. We understand them but they don't understand us. It makes life complicated for both sides.

At any rate, I now did what I often do—prowled

around the house until I came to a room in which I heard conversation and thereupon placed my forelegs on the windowsill and listened through the screen. Two-leggers call this eavesdropping, for some reason.

The sire was saying, "Do you happen to know the police number, my dear?"

"I don't. Just ask the operator and I think she'll connect you."

At that moment the phone rang.

"Yes," the sire said. "Speaking."

"Just who is this I'm talking to?" he asked.

"Now wait a minute," he said.

"Fifty thousand!" he said.

"In ten dollar bills," he said. "Yes, I understand."

"Unmarked," he said. "Now repeat those directions once again."

"You have my word for it. The police won't be notified," he said. "Now about Jeffrey. May I speak with him?"

"Oh, God, no," the dam kept saying over and over again in a tearful voice.

"Promise me then that you won't harm him," the sire said. A clicking sound followed. "Our son has been kidnapped." He spoke in a sad, flat tone. "I've got to get to the bank before it closes."

"Oh, our poor darling," the dam cried. "Who could do such an awful thing?"

"The voice was muffled," the sire said, "but somehow it sounded familiar."

"It's Carl," I barked. "The dirty dog-kicker."

They ignored me.

"I better get started," the sire said.

"I'll go with you," the dam said.

"I think you better remain here, in case there's another call. And don't breathe a word of this to Maude or anyone else. I'll be back with the money in about an hour."

"When will we get our baby back, dear?"

"I'm supposed to leave the money in a phone booth near Exit Seventy on the Connecticut Turnpike at exactly six o'clock tonight. We should have Jeff home for dinner."

A minute later the sire sped away in the squat car.

Depressed, I wandered back to the dogbane. Normally, I don't touch the milky sap, but this was not a normal occasion. I bit into a stem and chewed it to a sweet mushy pulp and swallowed. *Wow*, as they say.

Almost instantly my memory produced the powerful odor of sand flats. I could smell the wet kelp and the empty clam shells and the dead fish so sharply that when I looked around I was quite surprised not to see a wide expanse of salt water.

For a spell the sand-flat remembrance meant nothing to me. Then, as often happens among us canines on dogbane, a vision of the time and place came abruptly to mind. The time: this morning; the place: down at the end of the street. *I had smelled the sand flats on the tires of Carl's station wagon.*

In the name of Fido, I thought, here's a clue, a real honest-to-goodness clue. So, by Rover, let's act on it.

Without further ado I left the neighborhood and made for the sea. Within an hour I was getting a faint whiff of salt water. Ten minutes later I was standing on a sand dune and listening to the screeches of gliding gulls.

It's one whale of a lot of shoreline, I thought, so I'd better not waste any precious time.

I'd spent one entire summer of my life following the tides and feeding richly on fish, crabs and oysters. The area was not unfamiliar to me. I turned away from the sun and started my search. Behind me were fancy yacht clubs and private beaches. Ahead, as I recalled, were many empty expanses of marshland crisscrossed by tiny inlets, with an occasional marina to break the monotony and now and then a weather-beaten house standing shakily on a foundation of stilts. This was the type of geography I'd sniffed on the station-wagon wheels.

It was a long, hot afternoon. What little water I found to drink was brackish. I took a few swims to cool off but always I kept heading due east. I could tell by the slant of light that it was well past midafternoon and still I hadn't sniffed out my quarry. I did raise a brace of dreamy ducks while plunging through a canebreak, and a filthy white cat, its

arched back bristling, hissed at me from the shards
of an old skiff—but not one of my own kind
appeared at all.

Not in a long while have I spent such a fatiguing
afternoon. Only my abiding affection for Jeffrey
kept me going. Then, when I was nearly tempted to
curl up for a nap on a cool clump, I was rewarded. I
dug up, as we say, the big bone.

It happened as I was trudging up a sandy slope to
obtain a wider view of my immediate surroundings.
The sound of a motor starting up cut through the
heated stillness. I gazed northward, listening, nos-
trils alert. I soon discerned the top half of a station
wagon moving slowly behind a dune. I dropped
low on my belly and watched from between my
forelegs. Where the dune flattened out, the wagon
emerged. Carl, the booter of dogs, was at the wheel.
He was making slow and bumpy progress over a
narrow, deeply pitted road not much wider than a
sidewalk, and Jeffrey was not with him—he was not
visible to me, at least. In a few minutes the wagon
disappeared behind another dune in quest, obvi-
ously, of a better highway.

I promptly began to reconnoiter the grounds.
Within moments I caught Jeffrey's scent and followed it rapidly to a clapboard boathouse bleached
white by the wind and the sun and listing leeward
as if ready to collapse from the infirmities of old age.

Two-thirds of the boathouse rested on the beach, while the other third extended out over the water on piers of rock. I tackled it from the dry side. A fairly new duckwalk ran from the pitted road to a ramp of rotten wood. The ramp sagged up to an unpainted double door, which was secured by a shiny new padlock.

I explored the easterly side of the building. The walls were composed of decaying planks held together, it seemed, by the moods of the offshore breeze. There were apertures in some places as wide as my muzzle. I poked my nose into one of these. Jeffrey was there all right, but the interior gloom made him invisible.

Finally I barked—twice: "Jeff . . . ree."

"Big Dog," his small voice said, far off, from some remote corner of the place.

"Yes," I answered.

"I'm hungry," he said, a catch in his voice. "I want my mommy."

"Don't worry," I said, feeling no confidence. "I'll get her in a moment."

He began to cry then.

I scurried around to the western side of the building. There were no apertures there at all, just knotholes. Wading into the water, I swam out about a dozen feet and looked up. The seaward side of the boathouse presented a warped ramp raised to a crumbling roof. Functionally it was meant to be lowered into the water at high tide to make it easy to slide out a boat. Even if I could have leaped that high . . .

The tide was coming in, I noticed, as I paddled back to the spongy shore.

Well, there was only one thing left to do. I'd have to gnaw away at one of the apertures until it was large enough to let me crawl through.

Have you ever tasted desiccated wood on which sea worms have been feeding for decades? Probably not—and don't ever. Anyway, I gnawed for what seemed hours, slowly making headway, until I heard the station wagon approaching from the distance. Instantly I sought concealment behind a nearby clump of seaweed. The station wagon appeared a few moments later and came to a stop beside the duckwalk. Carl opened the door and got out. Before he closed the door again, I saw on the seat an attaché case and guessed that it contained the sire's money.

Carl walked to the padlocked door, taking a key from his pocket. Jeffrey was not crying now— maybe he'd fallen asleep. It was so quiet I could hear my own heartbeat. The click of the padlock opening was like a clap of thunder.

Carl swung the doors open—they sagged on their rusty hinges. He entered. I crept toward the ramp.

Inside it was still the color of dusk, but after a time I was able to see Carl's shadow moving through slats of light that leaked from the splits in the planking. And I saw Jeffrey too. He was a small bundle lying in a dark corner.

I inched inside the place and crawled silently toward a protective shadow. Jeffrey was crying softly again. I wanted to tell him I was close, but of course I couldn't.

Carl was operating some sort of squeaky device at the far end of the place—a pulley, as was soon proved—for suddenly the boat ramp separated from its juncture with the roof and began a creaking descent toward the water. Light poured in. I saw Jeffrey clearly now and he saw me. His hands and feet were bound together with rope. For a two-legger, he was pretty smart—smart enough not to say a word. As a result, Carl did not know I was there. His back was toward us and he was working away at a winch.

At that moment I was visited by a flash of insight. Carl was going to toss my small companion into the water and let him drown. With this conviction I got to my feet, all one hundred and twenty pounds of me. Jeffrey didn't call me Big Dog for nothing.

The ramp hit the water with a resounding splash. Carl began to turn just as I leaped forward. He saw me coming a second before I launched myself like a

missile into the air but it was too late for him to do
anything about it. I struck him hard in the chest. He
let out a gulping gasp and went over and out the
opening. I went with him, riding him like a surf-
board. We hit the lowered ramp first and then slid
swiftly down into the water. The tide was running
high now and Carl went under headfirst. I got off
and swam to the shore.

I stood there, shaking the water off my hide, and
waited for Carl to bob up. I waited quite a while. He
didn't appear. Satisfied at last, I ran back into the
boathouse and gnawed the ropes off Jeffrey's hands
and helped him with those around his ankles. He
was a tired and hungry boy, I tell you, but he
followed me out of there and up the pitted road
between the sand dunes and out onto the main
highway.

Almost right away we got a ride in a car driven by
a young female two-legger with a very kind voice.
She asked Jeffrey his name and wanted to know
what he was doing alone out on this road with night
coming on.

"I'm not alone," he told her. "I got Big Dog with
me." Then he tried to tell her what had happened,
but he wasn't very good at it and she didn't seem to
understand any of it. All she really got out of him
was his name and address—then she drove us
home.

Later that night Jeffrey tried to tell the story to his sire and dam, but they didn't believe much of it, particularly the part I played in it. They remained skeptical until the next morning when the police came to report that they had found the station wagon, the ransom money and Carl's body.

For lunch I had a sirloin steak all to myself. After that I walked around the garden with Jeffrey.

His sire and dam watched us from the gazebo.

"Mutt and Jeff," the sire said to the dam, and they laughed. They laughed a lot.